SIERA LONDON

I0677658

STAYING THE COURSE

The Men of Endurance

ABOUT THIS BOOK

Ivy Summer's poor choices have deposited her at the last knot in the proverbial rope. With forty dollars to her name and a broken shoe heel, she walks into the town of Endurance desperate and searching for a way back home. But this street-savvy lady is used to taking care of herself and fighting for everything she has. She'll do what's necessary to survive—even take on a grumpy mountain man in the middle of the night.

Single father, Owen Tate wants to be left alone, especially by the sexy trespasser who demands entry into his bar. She has a truckload of attitude, a penchant for manipulation, and a ton of baggage trailing behind her. Yet Ivy's zeal for life might be the kick in the pants a wounded man needs to bury the past.

How will two people used to staying the course change direction and learn to fight for each other?

STAYING THE COURSE

The Men of Endurance

Copyright © 2018 K. PRINGLE

Digital ISBN-13: 978-1-386376-07-1

Print ISBN-13: 978-1-949263-01-5

http://www.sieralondon.com[1]

Cover art by Fantasia Frog Designs

Edited by Gayla Leath, Dark Dreams Editing

Draft2Digital First Edition, June 2018

1.   http://www.siera

DEDICATION

THANK YOU TO AUTHOR, Olivia Gaines for contemplating a romance series about single fathers. Olivia gave me free rein to incorporate my small town of Endurance, featuring men getting a second chance at love, and voila, the Men of Endurance were born. Endurance is a unique place where we all can experience the beauty of an old fashion love story, rich friendships, and the blessing of family.

The town of Endurance is based on the city of Auburn, California, the endurance sports capital of the world. Throughout each book in the Men of Endurance series, you'll discover fun facts about Auburn and the rich history of Placer County.

To all my faithful readers, thank you from the bottom of my heart. You make this journey worthwhile. This book is dedicated to Carolyn D. Your little sister girlfriend loves you.

Blessings Romancelandia, Siera

CHAPTER ONE

The exclamation point at the end of Ivy Summers' streak of bad luck came three hours before midnight on a deserted stretch of California's Interstate 80.

How's about we do a little exchange? A ride for a ride.

Another gust of crisp wind slammed into her plastering her lightweight shirt against her chest. Battling the punishing cold was a small price compared to giving Ralph the Trucker a *ride*. With fingers stiff from the cold, she barely managed to hold onto her tattered backpack and gather the edges of her peeling second-hand leather jacket. The material felt smooth under her fingertips, the natural texture worn thin from wear and tear. Where was all this chill factor when the scorching June heat had melted the glob of school glue holding the heel of her combat boot in place? Though she'd been doing the stinky leg walk for miles, and her right calf ached from the uneven gait, the shoe fix took a back seat to her empty belly.

In the immediate future, she needed food, a crackling fire to drive the chill from her bones, and a quiet place to lay her head. Well, she could sleep on a theme park roller coaster at this point. When morning came, the first order of business would be a job, one that asked a short list of personal background questions and paid in long green cash. She'd stick around a few days to earn enough money to keep moving east... back to Shell Cove, Florida.

With every step, Ivy fought the urge to collapse under the weight of yet another bad decision. Following Johnny to California had been a mistake. Running from his brother Poe had been a calculated risk.

"Stay the course," she whispered. The mantra was a remnant of her time at the Second Chance women's shelter back in Shell Cove. "You can do it."

The warm light of civilization came into view, and Ivy breathed out a sigh of relief. Hungry, tired, and cold, she limped into the town of Endurance, California, population 1,333 per the marquee. In her guesstimation, the late-night interstate stroll had been at least four miles. Yet, she'd netted a big fat zero on the relief scale; zero all-night diners, zero truck stops, zero convenience stores, and zero motels. Either she'd stepped into the twilight zone, or the township had endured in the land that time forgot.

Ivy took a right off of Miramar Boulevard passing a fancy museum that housed the public library. At the town's center, a very regal looking City Hall building with a marble portico and an intricate pediment sat next to the sheriff's office, and then she came to a crossroads. How appropriate. She was at a crossroads with a lot of things in her life. She had a choice to make. Either she could go straight ahead onto Saratoga Springs or venture a little farther off the straight and narrow and take a right onto Miller Road. Would her destination hold more closed doors and dead ends?

From the intersection, the end of Saratoga Springs Road stared back at her. All of sudden, a sedan zoomed by, kicking up a cloud of road dust and pebbles.

"Hey," she railed, shielding her face with both hands, as she jumped out of the way. "Watch out, nut tart," she shouted to the vehicle's twin red lights. Coughing, she waved away the suffocating dirt swirl as the car disappeared from sight. Not wanting a close encounter of the deadly kind, she decided to avoid the road altogether.

"Alrighty then, Miller Road it is."

She passed Bee-Bee's bookstore. The quaint teal-colored stucco building had a neon sign shaped like a nineteen fifties coffee cup resting on a saucer. This was definitely a throwback town. Everyone knew coffee came in sixteen-ounce tall cups. The street was locked down tighter than a pill bottle in a nursing home. She wondered if this bargain bin Smallville even had a hotel, motel, or an Endurance Town Inn.

Prepared to give up and turn back, Ivy warmed when she saw a faint red glow coming from the far end of the street. Dragging her sore limbs forward, she approached the place with caution. There were velvet curtains at the two giant windows, the kind you might see at a fine restaurant known for patron privacy. The sign overhead the building read No Limit Bar and Grille. Looking back over her shoulder at the darkened street, she smirked. The town of Endurance definitely had a limit that probably didn't welcome wanderers like her. Ivy reached for the door handle and gave it a firm tug.

Nothing happened.

Giving it more muscle, Ivy gripped the faded wood, curling the fingers of both hands around the lever and yanked. On uneven heels, the added force and momentum had her wobbling on exhausted legs.

Still nothing.

Ivy felt the tears swell in her eyes. Don't cry. But, a familiar burn started in her nostrils, and then she felt the traitorous things flare in frustration. Dang it, she was going to cry. All of a sudden, the door flew open. Before she knew it, her body was in motion, flying backwards, and her behind hit the cobblestone road, hard.

"Crap," she grumbled, followed by a few choice swear words as she sat on the ground, contemplating her misfortune. It seemed she had an invisible bad luck symbol etched on her forehead.

A guy, a blonde haired mountain with steel blue eyes glared down at her, his height imposing from this position. She tried to stop her eyes from taking a walk up his impressive form. Cowboy boots, darkened with age, covered his large feet. Denim jeans, not too tight, not too loose, clung to legs defined with muscle. His thighs looked like he could support her weight for hours and not tire. A plaid shirt, buttoned up the front, did little to conceal his broad shoulders and sculpted abdomen. Yep, those pecs could be in one of those Sleep-Right commercials. Every woman she knew would claw her best friend's eyes out to have a chest like his cradling her head.

"We're closed," he growled, face locked in a stony expression.

She waited for him to extend a hand to help her up. After all, it had been his fault that she fell.

She waited some more. Okay, still nothing. Rubbing her hands together to rid them of the ground debris, she winced as loose gravel scraped across her abraded palms. She looked up at ole blue eyes.

"Your sign says you're open," she said, removing her backpack.

He gave the sign a cursory glance, and then frowned. "I'm not." He bobbed his chin in her direction. "You're trespassing."

Unless there was a new ordinance expanding the trespassing law to include sitting on your butt in a public street, he was wrong. Ivy came to her feet, no thanks to him. Looking up, she craned her neck. Whoa, he was tall, and kind of cute in a small-town Scrooge way.

"Then you should turn the lights off," she said with a scowl.

He gave her a twisted smirk. "You from the bank?"

She reared back, staring up at him in confusion. Dressed in her best pair of ripped jeans and a University of California sweatshirt she'd grabbed off a Goodwill clearance rack in Imperial Beach, there was nothing business-like about her. Why, in her current state of dress, he would think she was from the bank confused her even more.

"Nope," she told him, adding a bit of sass to her tone.

He grinned, baring his teeth. Scary, but going without Maslow's hierarchy of needs frightened her more.

"Then, don't tell me what to do, lady."

Her stomach growled, and he narrowed his eyes on her. When it screamed out again, the blue-eyed grumpy-pants stepped onto the sidewalk peering down at her. He looked up the street, examining the dark shadows where she'd come from.

"Where's your car?"

Her eyes widened in surprise at his question. This morning, she'd hitched a ride outside of a San Diego rest area with an overweight trucker named Ralph headed to San Francisco with a trailer load of garlic bulbs. Eight hours into the trip he confessed to never having slept with a woman of her persuasion. He spewed some nonsense about her reminding him of a lovely black unicorn, and then proceeded to grope her with his sausage-sized fingers. When the heck had Ralph the trucker ever seen a unicorn? Maybe, the pervert had puffed some of Cali's medical marijuana. Either way, Ivy had screamed for him to stop the rig, giving little attention to the where and when as she exited the semi-truck.

"What?" she managed to stammer.

"Where," he drawled, his voice deliciously deep with a masculine base, "is your car?"

She looked around. Nervous energy started to bubble in her gut. Okay, she was alone, in some one-traffic light town, with a suddenly angry bar owner towering over her. Maybe she should have tested her luck back in the truck with the last black unicorn hunter.

"I walked," she confessed, acutely aware of her vulnerable circumstance.

He kept his eyes on her. "The five miles from the highway?"

He practically growled the words. And now, Ivy was officially scared.

She lifted her chin, speaking with more confidence than she felt. "Walking through God's country never hurt anybody."

He stared at her. And on a stack of hotel bibles, she could have sworn she saw fire roar in his eyes.

"At night it can," he snapped, but a cord of sadness hung on each word.

A mountain of pain erupted in those telling eyes, but then it vanished. Something much harder and menacing replaced it. Okay, time to put some distance between her and blue-eyed hell boy.

"Look," she said, slowly inching back. "I was looking for some food. I saw the sign but—I'm really sorry I disturbed you, sir."

As she talked, Ivy inched further away, putting distance between his body and hers in case she needed to pull a 'don't-go-into-the-woods scream' and run down Miller Road. Then, the oddest thing happened.

He smiled. "I'm sir now?"

The smile, the eyes, the body all worked for her. He truly was a handsome grumpy pants.

"I'll call you whatever you want," she swallowed. Psycho alert, she thought.

Ivy gazed at the darkening street ahead. She could make a break for it. With a hint of luck, she might make it back to the highway. Just then, a child appeared in the doorway, rubbing his eyes with small balled up fists.

"Daddy, what's taking you so long? I'm ready for my bedtime story."

A little boy with straw-colored hair, lighter than his father's, pushed a half-hidden torso from behind one of those long legs. He wore an Ironman sleep romper that covered his feet and zipped up to his neck. It looked like there was a cape or something behind him, but in the low light it was hard for Ivy to tell.

"Go back inside, Cai," he told the child.

At least, the kid was interested in books, rather than video games. It was the first indication that the man was human after all.

"Who are you talking to?" the child demanded.

She couldn't hide the shock on her face. Mr. Grumpy Pants had produced a little demanding version of himself.

"Nobody," he said in his firm father's voice.

Ivy gritted her teeth. Now, why did he have to go and say a thing as bone-headed as that? It almost hurt her feelings that he equated her presence to a non-entity. She had been discounted most of her life. No way would she permit this stranger to deem her invisible.

The same blue eyes as his fathers regarded her, and she thought she heard Mr. Grumpy Pants say the boy's name was Kyle. The little sleepy head reached for his father's giant hand.

The child asked, "Who's that lady?"

"Cai, I said—," the man interjected.

Ivy interrupted. She could feel his eyes on her, intense and scrutinizing. Looking at Cai, she ignored the father. True, it was beneath her to use a child to save her own hide, but her belly and body had reached their limit.

"Hello Cai. My name is Ivy Summers."

He laughed. "That's a pretty name." He shook his daddy's hand, capturing his attention. "Isn't her name pretty, Daddy?"

Grumpy Pants' frown deepened. "It's alright."

She scowled back. She didn't know what his problem was, and she didn't care. She needed food. That's when she felt strong fingers grip her elbow. Ivy squeezed her eyes shut prepared for a crushing pain. Instead, warmth, tingling, and an 'oh so delicious' sensation wound its way up her arms. His fingers contracted where they touched, and then relaxed. Had he felt it too?

"Come inside, Ivy. I'll feed you," he said in that deep sexy tone.

That voice was already feeding something wicked inside of her. A lingering hunger she'd neglected to feed for a long while salivated at his deep timbre. She'd have to make sure to keep quiet over whatever meal he put in front of her. The last thing Ivy needed was his voice distracting her from a full belly.

"Are you sure your wife will be okay with me grabbing a quick bite before moving on?"

When he didn't answer, she looked up to find him watching her again. His eyes were doing that dancing fire thing once more as he took her all in.

"She's not here," he said, his voice dropped low and somehow vacant sounding.

Ivy pulled up short. Married men were a hard limit for her. She wasn't looking for any trouble, yet the way his eyes drank in her features before settling on her mouth, she got the impression that food was the last thing on his mind.

WHEN was the last time she'd eaten? Owen watched from the doorway as Ivy polished off a second bowl of bowtie pasta, before she added a third chicken leg to her plate. At this late hour, a woman in the house signaled an exciting turn of events for Cai. Owen had to carry his son up the stairs to keep him from bombarding their strikingly beautiful houseguest with questions, the first of which focused on her 'broken' shoe. Ivy had smiled at Cai's inquiry, but Owen noticed she tucked her tattered footwear farther under the table, out of sight. The kitchen table, square shaped with four sturdy armless chairs, had been with him since college. He and Jose, a local builder, had designed the kitchen remodel themselves and done most of the work. The picture window above the sink looked big enough to step through and provided an unobstructed view of Tommy's Park and the surrounding forest.

Ivy had removed her ratty old UC sweatshirt and gotten comfortable the moment he placed a plate in front of her. The contrast between her sienna brown skin and the bright starburst tie-dye shirt struck him like sunrise after a year-long black out. Curls, rich with colors of cocoa, cinnamon, and ebony hung in thick coils at her shoulders. Her nose was pert, and her lips were so lush, he wished he was that fork she kept sliding into her mouth. Delicious for sure. She was a petite woman, but curvy. Her hips, more than a handful, looked like she could give a man the ride of his life. Her waist, though trim, had some womanly fullness. Definitely, not skin and bones. It had been a long time since he'd seen a woman with her type of figure in Endurance.

The town, known for extreme sports, catered to the lean athletic type with their designer-priced sports bras for chests with less definition than his, and hips so lean they could step through a Cheerio with room to spare. His late wife, Caitlyn had considered herself plump compared to most women in town. She'd been perfect, even after she held onto a pound or two from giving birth to Cai. Yeah, Owen liked his women soft and shapely, like Ivy Summers. Heck, even her name was soft and feminine. The woman radiated warmth and life. And those whiskey-colored eyes, seductive in their almond shape, missed little. Case in point, he looked up to find her regarding him.

"Does Cai's father have a name?"

He shot her a look of warning. "Owen Tate."

Owen watched as she reached for the near empty lemonade pitcher, then hesitated, before she seemed to remember she was a guest.

"Would it be okay if I finished this off, Owen?"

"Go ahead," he nodded, "but, slow down. There's more."

Her back stiffened. Slowly, she pulled the napkin from her lap and wiped her mouth.

"Thank you for the meal." Without looking at him, she came to her feet. "Where's the closest hotel?"

So, he'd wounded the little minx's pride. Owen knew how it felt to have something you wanted so close, yet not be able to enjoy it. He'd been down and out as a kid. It was one of the things that had led him to the military, and eventually on to college.

"You running from something?"

She looked around her feet, and then gave him a twisted grin. "Not at the moment."

Did she have a smart comment for every question? There were a lot of reasons a woman would be walking alone at night, and none of them were good. And, nobody found Endurance without somehow being bumped and bruised along the way. He wondered at Ivy Summers' story.

"Look," he said, grabbing another carton of lemonade from the freezer. "I got a four-year-old who needs his father alive and well. So, is trouble after you?"

The prettiest shade of crimson flushed her cheeks, before she admitted, "Not tonight, he isn't."

Fear flashed in her eyes, then as if a female warrior had taken hold, a fierce scowl covered her features. So, she was in trouble.

"This trouble got a name?" Growing up in these mountains, Owen learned to track, hunt, wrestle...heck, he could defend himself against just about anybody. A four-year stint serving his country in the United States Navy had perfected his skills, but that didn't mean he wanted to use them anytime soon.

"I'm moving on, remember?"

Placing the frosty container in the sink to thaw, he wiped his damp fingers on a bar cloth. Where was she planning to 'move on' to? It was Sunday night and the traffic along Interstate-80 would be at a minimum. Did she plan to hitch another ride out of town? It was none of his business, but that never stopped him in the past.

"Where are you headed to?"

"Oh, here, there, and everywhere," she said giving him the biggest fake smile.

At twenty-nine, he was too old for games. He growled his displeasure.

"So, you're wandering the mountains of Northern California at night, without a clue as to where you're going? How old are you?" Owen tried to curtail his condemning tone. Maybe, with a full belly his admonition would go unnoticed.

Though she pretended to be aloof, he knew she noticed because that slim back of hers rounded like a cat about to strike.

"Legal," she said, face darkening with ferocity. "It's getting late. I'll be going now."

He pushed off the doorframe, standing to his full height. "Finish eating, first."

"I'm full. The hotel?" she repeated.

So, she thought it okay to challenge a man in his own house? He had a right mind to bend her over his knee. Trying to get the little minx to eat shouldn't be a crime.

"Sit. Eat," he snapped.

He knew he'd messed up the moment the words left his fool lips. She crossed her shapely arms over a petite torso, lean and toned probably from working. He couldn't see the size of her breasts, but those hips filled out her jeans. Ivy Summers met his stare.

"No," she said, not backing down.

He stalked towards her. "You about ripped the door off the hinges to get to some food. Now, eat." He let authority seep into his voice.

The woman turned towards the table, and a thread of disappointment wormed through him that she'd backed down so quickly. He found he liked sparring with her. It didn't make sense. Owen ran the bar and focused on raising a son, who would grow into a man that his mother would be proud of. An occasional round of golf with Abel Burney, the golf course owner and beers with the fellas...he didn't talk with women...ever. Caitlyn had been *it* for him. Yet here he was, yucking it up with Ivy. Dang, her name was pretty. Owen's pulse skipped when she folded the napkin he'd given here, gathered up the used dishes, and took them to the sink.

"What are you doing?" It surprised him because she thought to lighten his load. And, he wasn't sure why he'd pulled down the China for her. Caitlyn, his late wife, had loved decorating the dinner table, said it made her feel like she was taking care of her family. They hadn't used this stuff since the Christmas after Cai's third birthday...since Caitlyn's death. So, what did it say about him preserving the memory of his wife for Cai's benefit? "You don't have to clean up," he pushed out. Once again she ignored him.

Most nights, he fed Cai from some superhero-themed paper plate. His kid lived and breathed Marvel's Ironman. As for the floral print linen napkin, he and Cai had no use for the fancy cloth he'd placed under her fork and knife. If he didn't know himself better, he'd think he was trying to impress her. Owen didn't have an impressive bone in his body. Outside of the bedroom, he wasn't that good at wooing a woman.

"I'm ready to leave now," she said, chin lifted. Owen saw her eyeing the backpack that looked like she swiped it off a trash pile. "I've got forty-dollars." She shook her head as if she'd disclosed a detail that would threaten national security. "How much do I owe you?"

He couldn't let her walk out of here. Walking these deserted stretches of highway were dangerous. Besides, there wasn't a hotel room available for another hundred miles. Did she know anything about Endurance? It was race season from now till October. The hotels were booked out for months.

He narrowed his eyes. "Don't want your money."

Without thinking he took another look at that body of hers. Ivy knowing exactly what he was doing, took a step back.

But, it was her fear that pricked at his protective instinct. Owen didn't like that she was afraid. She was too pretty to be afraid.

Well, the scowl darkened the image, but Owen had that effect on others.

"You can stay here," he offered.

"I'm not going to wake up to find you butt naked in my room with a cup of vanilla pudding and a bottle of Viagra, am I?"

Owen stared at the tiny slip of a woman asking him if he was a pervert. When he didn't answer, the area between her brows slipped into fierce 'v'. She was serious.

He gave her an answer.

"Chocolate's my favorite. Don't need Viagra," he stated, voice flat.

The scowl deepened. "I can defend myself, so you'd better be joking."

Now, she was ready to take him out if necessary? Who was this spitfire he'd invited into his home?

"You got thirty seconds to decide." Baring his teeth, Owen looked his late-night caller in those beautiful brown eyes. "What's it going to be, sweetheart."

"I'll take the room, minus the pudding and the sweetheart comments."

"Ivy," he said, trying to add a reassuring tone to his voice. "I'm not asking for anything."

"Oh yeah," she challenged. "Those pretty midnight blues of yours are doing a whole lot of window shopping. You think you were getting some of my chocolate kisses because you fed me?"

She was right, but he was in no mood to apologize for noticing a beautiful woman. He braced his legs apart and crossed his arms over his chest.

"You're pretty," he growled. "And if I did take you to bed, I'd want a helluva lot more than a kiss."

She growled back at him. "You're pretty too, but you don't see me stripping you butt naked with my eyes."

Had she just admitted she found him tempting? The little vixen was as bold as her tie-dye shirt.

She reached for the backpack, and he was on her in seconds.

God, she smelled sweet. A combination of wild flowers, cool breeze, and warm woman. What the heck was Ivy Summers doing to him? Literally, he'd been dead inside his jeans until she fell on that luscious ass at his feet. One look at her and he knew he shouldn't touch her. But something in those beautiful brown doe eyes called to his protective instinct. An instinct that he no longer ignored. Ivy Summers definitely needed a man's protection and there was no way he'd let her leave. Not tonight.

"Let go," she hissed.

He looked down to find his hand locked over hers. They both held the strap of the backpack in a standoff.

"You're not walking anywhere in the middle of the night." He tightened his jaw. Maybe, he should try another approach. He would use the whole more flies with honey analogy, though he for sure didn't want any flies from Ivy Summers. "Ivy, I have a room upstairs."

Those eyes he liked gazing in widened, and then her pink tongue glided across her lips. Owen, the simpleton that he was, leaned in closer. What would she taste like?

"I'm not a whore." He noticed she balled her hands into fists.

"Glad to hear it," he drawled, tone relaxed, "seeing as I can't have you plying your wares in front of my four-year old."

Her eyes narrowed. "Plying what?" she huffed. "I'm not trading any flesh for food, that's the point I was making."

"And here I was falling prey to all your simpering purrs and seductive banter," he scoffed. "Shut up woman, and finish your food. And, what happened to your shoe?"

She stared at him, as if she were seeing him for the first time. "Are you gay?"

Her hickory eyes called to him, but her sharp tongue...the things they could do.

"Why? Feeling rejected?"

"Of course not. Well, you could pretend a little interest."

He burst out laughing. There was no pleasing this woman.

"Whatever," she snapped.

"Precisely. You staying or going?"

She hesitated, then asked. "Where's your wife?"

Now it was Owen's turn to hesitate. "My wife, Caitlyn, died almost two years ago."

It shocked and awed him when sadness filled her eyes.

"Oh, I'm so sorry, Owen," she whispered. "I'll stay," she paused, "as long as we're clear my pudding is not for sampling."

What was it with the food references? And why the heck was his mouth watering?

"Thanks," he muttered, not wanting her pity. He could smell the food he'd prepared clinging to her. A little sweet, and a whole lot of spice. Shoot, if that wasn't the woman in front of him. "It's just an extra bed," and then he added, "the door has a lock."

She swallowed. Her eyes darted away from his. He found he missed her eyes on him.

"How much?" she asked.

Did everything come down to dollars and cents with this woman? He thought about that avalanche that had sounded in her stomach and the few belongings in that threadbare backpack. Actually, she didn't have on much clothing for the cool that settled over the desert this time of year. If he told her the room was free of charge, she would wrestle with him for the next thirty minutes over the charitable act. Though he welcomed the company, Cai was upstairs alone. With Owen talking away downstairs, he was sure his inquisitive four-year-old was still awake.

"Tonight is free. Tomorrow you pay."

He knew she'd refuse if she thought he offered an open-ended invitation. Life had dealt Ivy Summers a near death blow, yet she stood, poised for the next strike. The walk hadn't broken her, and the night hadn't frightened her. Ivy Summers was a trained soldier in the war of hard knocks, a true survivor.

"Who said I'll be here tomorrow?" she mumbled, but he heard her. Owen almost smiled at her cry of courage.

He'd said it. His heart twisted at the thought of her out on the road to nowhere alone, vulnerable. Almost two years widowed, Owen accepted that this was his path to walk, raising his son alone, and he'd stay the course, but ... Ivy would stay the night. The sudden urge he felt to keep her safe and under his roof pissed him off. He belonged to Caitlyn, heart and soul, yet his fingers ached to touch Ivy Summers one more time.

CHAPTER TWO

Ivy wondered at the sudden change in Owen's mood. He'd practically forbid her to leave, but now he sulked as if he were upset she'd stayed. Was it a mistake to accept his offer to bunk down for the night? As they traversed to a back staircase off the kitchen, he'd been angry...at her. In the morning, she'd hit the pavement at sunrise.

She was safe and well-fed...for now.

Owen opened the door. "This is the room."

He angled his large frame, giving her a narrow passage. Her arm brushed his abdomen and she felt the contraction of his muscles vibrate through her body. Her breath caught. This tension between them was off the charts.

"Thanks," she said, slipping past him.

The bedroom was small in size containing a full-size bed with a lacy-white bedskirt. Yep, a woman had been here. "It's pretty."

Owen grunted something about not his doing. While she took in her temporary home, he hung back by the door.

There was one window. Beyond the trees behind the bar, she could just make out the outline of the mountain range. A small table sat with two silver picture frames. In one photo, Owen wore a cap and gown. Above his smiling face the printed words University of California stood out next to the letters

MBA. The next frame held a family portrait. Owen stood behind an upholstered chair, a blonde woman held an infant that Ivy assumed was Cai. His wife looked polished and dainty, attributes Ivy lacked. Suddenly, she felt like an intruder. *Leave,* she thought.

"Ivy?" Owen said, a note of concern in his voice.

She tightened her grip on the backpack. This man and his son didn't need her storming into their domesticated lives. What did she know about white lace and family portraits? Poe would keep searching for her. What if he hurt Owen, or worse yet, Cai? A guilty conscience would make a restful sleep unlikely.

"Ivy." His deep timbre filling the small room. "What is it?"

She felt the heat of his hand before it settled on her shoulder. When had he moved away from the door? Even with her back to him, she struggled to keep the slow burn his touch sparked from spreading in a very foolhardy direction. So much about him overwhelmed her.

"Nothing," she squeaked out, glancing over her shoulder. Owen looked down at the pack in her hand, and then back at her. Could he see her internal struggle? Forty dollars might get her a room for the night.

"Give me your pack, Ivy," he whispered.

He made it sound simple. *Come on little lady spend one night in the belly of temptation to test your mettle.* On a sigh, she handed it over.

"Here." This decision would probably leave a painful bruise. She was definitely leaving in the morning. Owen dropped the pack in the chair none too gently.

"Get some rest," he told her. "I'm up at six."

Was that his way of telling her to have her stuff packed?

"Understood." A lie. She didn't understand not one thing since she'd laid eyes on Owen Tate. Her brain and her body, were both in some wonderland of sensation that she couldn't process with him so close.

The other hand settled on her left shoulder. Slowly he turned her to face him.

"Tell me what you understand."

Heat, masculine and consuming, surrounded her. The gentle wave washed over her, driving the chill from her limbs. During the walk into Endurance, she'd repeated words of encouragement she learned as a child at the Second Chance House to distract her from the cold. Somehow hearing herself recite the familiar phrases centered her. Yeah, it wasn't working. Owen Tate's nearness was crossing wires and scrambling all kinds of brain circuits. She had shelter for the night. That had to be enough. No romantic notions allowed.

"I'll be back on the highway tomorrow."

He mumbled a couple of words before she heard a gruff, "We'll see."

What? She was too tired to fend off this emotional jeopardy match they had going on.

Owen's lips thinned. Okay, why did her saying she'd be on her way seem to piss him off more?

"Breakfast is at seven-thirty," he said, gaze unflinching, and then he disappeared to the other side of the door.

"We'll see," she mimicked, sticking her tongue out at the closed door. Why did she get the feeling Owen Tate enjoyed rattling her cage? The man was insufferable, and she was behaving like a spoiled brat.

Crossing the room, she opened the largest zipped compartment on her pack. Digging through, she pulled out her phone and cord charger. Early in her travels, she'd learned to keep her phone juiced. Hitching a ride was okay, but she kept her bags closed and close. She found a power outlet hidden behind soft drapes, the color of midday sunshine. With a sudden stir of nerves, Ivy waited until the icon disappeared before hitting the text message symbol. Reading the accumulated messages, she released a sigh of relief. Nothing from Poe. Maybe, he'd decided against searching for her.

Stumbling to the bed, Ivy collapsed in exhaustion. Was a fresh start too much to hope for? When she closed her eyes, she could feel the movement of the treadmill that was her life. If she could put some distance between her, the robbery, and Poe, maybe she could get back home and rebuild her life instead of running but getting nowhere.

She thought of Owen watching her eat. When he looked at her, she felt different, reborn somehow. His eyes seemed to touch her everywhere. A tingling started low in her belly the instant he touched her. Those blue eyes, she'd seen them darken to a thunderous cobalt when he grabbed her backpack. Whoa, she was expending too much energy thinking about Owen Tate.

"Get up," she mumbled to herself. With a groan she pushed herself to stand on tired feet.

With her toiletry bag and sleep shirt in tow, she opened the bedroom door. Owen had left the light on for her. Sweet guy, for a grump. A quick shower first, and then off to la-la land.

The bathroom, with its lively yellow walls, reminded Ivy of sunflowers. In lieu of a bathtub, there was a shower with dual heads on one wall. A small oval sink sat in a white cabinet with fancy brushed gold fixtures. The toilet was the fanciest thing in the room. Instead of a handle, the contraption had two silver buttons that fit together like one of those black and white peace symbols. This place reeked of a woman's touch, yet Owen Tate seemed too hard for this woman's soft lace and brushed gold. Ivy shook herself. When had she become an Owen Tate aficionado? He was the polar opposite of the rough necks she usually rolled with.

Ten minutes later carrying her Ziploc bag filled with lotion, deodorant, toothpaste, a folding tooth brush, and baby powder, she stepped into the hallway and bumped into a sleepy eyed four year-old.

Cai looked up, and stumbled back as if he were scared.

Whoa. The kid wasn't used to seeing her in his space. His reaction answered one of her questions. Owen Tate, if he had a lady friend, kept his *company* separated from his son.

Eager to allay his fears, Ivy dropped to her knees.

"Cai, it's Ivy. Remember me?"

He approached, caution in his padded step. "I'm four. I got...good memory."

Okay, he was just as direct as his father. Owen's wife must have had her hands full with these two yahoos.

She tousled his hair. "Of course you do, sweetheart."

He frowned. "Boys aren't sweethearts."

She guessed not. Ivy changed the subject. "What are you doing out of the bed?"

That seemed to get him focused on his reason for being in the hallway. "The light in the potty 'posed to stay on."

She slapped a palm against her forehead. Of course. Owen had left the light on for his son. Again, she wasn't thinking clearly.

Ivy took Cai by the hand. She'd just flipped the light on, and closed the bathroom door behind him when she felt a presence behind her.

Spinning on bare feet, she slammed into a bare-chested Owen. In the dark, he seemed even larger, more menacing. Before she could back away, he captured her around the waist. Awareness of their intimate contact spiked through her. Male heat and hard muscle sent her pulse racing faster than a thoroughbred.

"Everything okay?"

Her eyes widened. Talk about the land of hard plains and rippled valleys.

"Yeah," she whispered, body pressed against Owen's taut abs. *Warning,* a little voice echoed in her head, *entering the Twilight Zone.* Long ago, Ivy stopped listening to her inner voice once that voice had convinced her that life on the back of Johnny's bike would be better than living alone. Now, Johnny was gone. Ivy was on her own, and Poe expected to collect on Johnny's debt. And that little inner voice, well, that heifer was a big liar.

OWEN woke up stony as a riverbed with a mood to match. One night with Ivy under his roof and he'd had to exercise every advanced control technique the military had taught him. Finding her in the hallway last night in another one of her tie-dye shirts, and nothing else, was more temptation than a saint could bear. And man, once her touched her, there was nothing saintly about his thoughts. That slow burn he'd felt at the first touch erupted into a five-alarm fire. Every part of him was hankering for more.

Holding Ivy in his arms, reminded Owen of how long it had been since he'd caressed a woman. He remembered how much he missed Caitlyn. But, it wasn't his wife that occupied his dreams. Nope, it was a little spitfire with wild curls and a sharp tongue. He knew the fire Ivy lit beneath his skin would blaze for months, maybe even years. She was wrong about the pudding and Viagra, but boy howdy, he could have gazed at her all night. Be that as it may, he found himself looking forward to breakfast. Would Ivy wear another one of those color burst t-shirts or would she surprise him?

"Stop being a sap," he muttered. He had about twenty minutes to ready breakfast, feed Cai, and pass on instructions to Delaney, his morning help.

Mornings were crisp in the Sierra Nevada foothills until the mid-morning sunshine burned off the humidity. This morning was more of the same.

"Daddy, the toast," Cai chirped from his booster seat at the dinette table.

"Shoot," Owen mumbled, grabbing the charred bread from the quad toaster with his fingers. "Thanks, buddy."

Most of downstairs consisted of the bar, the patron dining room, and a commercial-grade kitchen with a food storage pantry. To keep Cai from eating in the bar and overhearing adult conversations that he would ask about later, Owen had added a family living area with a simple yet functional dining, an L-shaped kitchen with custom cabinets above a farmhouse sink, and a television room for their private use. Caitlyn had loved the new addition with its open concept design.

Cai shook his head. "Where's Ms. Delaney?"

Blowing on his fingers, Owen scraped the top layer off revealing a thin white section beneath. "On her way," he rasped, hoping today it would be the truth.

Delaney had a promising future being the high school's valedictorian and all. But, the summer before college she'd met some semi-professional athlete in town for one of the endurance races and had fallen in love. Four years gone, and she was still waiting on Dillon, something or other, to come back and take her away from small town life. Betty Jo, her Grammy, had been like a mother to Caitlyn, so Owen had offered the lost young woman a job. Owen hadn't expected Delaney to be a star employee, but he never anticipated how apathetic Delaney was about her lack of performance. He placed a lidded Ironman cup filled with whole milk and a piece of toast in front on Cai.

"Eat up, Cai."

"'Kay. Will Ms. Autumn be ere after school?" he asked with his mouth full.

Autumn was a local college student looking to earn some extra bucks in between semesters. A year ago, when she'd approached him about babysitting Cai, he'd welcomed the help. Without Caitlyn, Owen had been scrambling to manage the bar with a rambunctious three-year-old under foot. Owen suspected Autumn's financial situation might be more dire than she let on, but she always refused his offer of an advance on her pay. Usually, Autumn made Cai's afternoon snack and got him off to bed, so Owen could focus on getting the late-night noise makers, usually students from UC Endurance, out of the bar so he could close up shop.

"Ms. Autumn may even pick up you from school today." Last night's receipts needed to be deposited at 1st Bank.

Owen thought of Ivy's shapely arms as she tried to enter the bar last night. He shook his head. Stubborn woman, she didn't quit. Owen found himself smiling. Where was she? He glanced in the direction of the back stairs. Should he check on Ivy? When he'd come downstairs her bedroom door remained closed, thank heaven. Another peak at those thick legs, and he'd probably burn another batch of toast.

Opening the back door, to rid the room of charred bread odor, Owen glanced at the clock.

"Delaney," he muttered, grabbing Cai's book bag from the back of a table chair. This morning's customers would have to wait. Cai needed to get to school. He swore under his breath. More money lost to Della's Diner or the new coffee house, High Altitudes. The money he made during tourist season kept the bills paid through the lean months. He needed to make a decision about Delaney...and soon.

"Come on, buddy. Time for school."

Cai frowned. "But...but, Ms. Delaney's not here."

The sound of light footsteps approaching drew his attention. Ivy, dressed in skinny jeans and another multi-colored shirt, stood with her backpack over one shoulder. She looked nervous.

"Sorry...I, I overslept."

The look on her face said she expected a sharp comment. Instead Owen told her the truth.

"Glad you slept well."

A man liked to know his woman felt safe under his protection. Whoa. That was a loaded thought. Nothing about Ivy Summers belonged to him. And why did that unsettle his gut? The woman needed to belong to somebody. Plenty of hitchhikers meet with hell's minions in God's country. Owen wasn't so naive to think every small town served as a safe haven for vulnerable women. Quite the opposite, especially for one as beautiful as Ivy. "There's juice, coffee, and toast."

She dropped the backpack at the foot of the stairs. Owen had the sudden urge to haul the thing to the trash. Then she'd stay.

"Sounds great. Who are Delaney and Autumn?"

Man, she didn't argue when it came to food. A desert breeze swooped in through the open door, ruffling wisps of hair around her face. The loose curls gone, instead she wore thick twists that hung down to her shoulders. He liked the look on her.

"Delaney serves as my waitress. Autumn is Cai's babysitter," he answered, unable to take his eyes off her. "I like your hair like that."

In an uncharacteristically shy move, Ivy ducked her head. Again, a rosy glow bloomed in her cheeks. Interesting. Comments on her sex appeal were met with bold innuendo, but a compliment earned him a blush.

"Thank you, Owen," she smiled, crossing the floor to the counter.

Owen chuckled when Ivy crinkled her nose at the burnt toast on the plate. Looking around, she started opening cupboards, until she spied what she sought. With a coffee cup in hand, she poured a full cup, and took a pull.

"Hmmm, that's good." She took her time, touching every-thing on the counter, the utensil caddy, the spoon holder, the mug rack, and then she stopped at the sink. Her gaze fixed on the view.

"Wow." Her face split into a wide grin, child-like and cute as all get-out. "It's beautiful here."

Owen stood a little bit taller, knowing he'd given her some-thing she wouldn't find anywhere else...the raw beauty of small town living in the foothills.

He walked up behind her, careful not to touch.

"That big tree to your left is a Valley Oak. Beyond that, the tall ones that look like Christmas trees are Ponderosa and Jeffery Pines. The central valley is full of them. As you move further up the mountains, there's so many Douglas Firs, you'd think you were one of Santa's elves."

"Oh, can I be an elf, Daddy?" Cai chimed in.

Ivy turned in the cradle of his arms.

"I've never seen a place so beautiful, Owen." She beamed up at him, awe in her voice.

"Know just how you feel, sweetheart," he said, smoothing a few hairs back from her forehead. "Beautiful," he whispered. Neither of them moved, yet the room seemed to be spinning around them.

"Y'come you keep staring at Ivy, Daddy?"

Ivy's breath hitched. He recognized the instant the spell was broken.

"Yeah, Daddy," she smirked, "Why you keep looking?" she teased, lifting her half-full cup to pink lips, and taking a sip.

Clearing his throat, Owen took a step back.

"Eat something, Ivy." He couldn't bring himself to say, "before you leave."

"That toast is darker than me," she frowned. "I'll pass."

Cai, mouth filled with his piece said, "Daddy said men like their toast bar-b-q."

Owen felt heat rush to his face. Cai's reasoning wasn't meant for public consumption. Ivy regarded him with raised brows.

"Bar-B-Q toast, ah yeah. That's got to be a violation of some type of commandment, Owen."

Before he could explain himself, the house phone rang.

"No Limit," he barked. Delaney sounded frantic on the other end of the line. "Slow down, honey. What's wrong?"

Owen listened, while frustration bubbled in his gut. He expected late, not absent.

"What's wrong?" Ivy mouthed.

The now empty coffee cup sat on the counter. A metal slide, then pop sounded in the background. Two slices of toast, golden in their perfection, and slathered with butter and strawberry jam appeared on the table. She cut them into two halves. Cai didn't need an invitation. His son grabbed the slice and ate greedily. In a surprise move, she walked over to him and held up a slice. Keeping his eyes on her, he grabbed the warm sweetness between his teeth. Her breath hitched, and her pupils dilated to Frisbees. He listened to Delaney explain that she had injured her wrist in a fall, all the while watching Ivy.

He hung up the phone and ran a hand through his hair. What was he supposed to do without a cook and a waitress?

Ivy dusted her palms together ridding them of greasy crumbs. Would Ivy stay if he asked? He should let her go, but he needed her. Plus, he wanted her with him...for her safety, of course.

Looking at his son, Owen swallowed his trepidation and asked, "I need help. My waitress, Delaney, can't come in today." He waited, hoping she'd jump right in with an offer to help. "I wondered if I gave you some money, maybe?" He was mucking this up. Just ask her, you big lug. Thank goodness, she saw fit to rescue him.

"You offering me a job, Owen Tate?"

He ground his teeth. Was he? "Maybe." Yes.

"Then maybe I need room and board, before I answer."

"Done," he pointed a finger in her direction. "What else?"

She hesitated. "I need to earn one-hundred dollars a day...half in cash and half transferred to a Venmo account." He was just about to say done, but then she added. "Nightly."

That pulled him up short. Did someone depend on her for money? He could tell there was more. She glanced at Cai, and Owen stiffened. What was she about to say?

She leaned in close. "I'm not sleeping with you," she whispered.

Bed sports sure did come up in her conservations a lot.

"I remember," he whispered back in jest. Before she could suspect his next move, he strolled over to the stairs, and snatched up her backpack.

"Hey, put that back," she protested.

"Afterwards," he said plucking his keys from the hook by the door.

"After what?"

"You get to work," he grinned. "Time for school, Cai. Let's get a move on."

He headed out the door with Cai in one arm and Ivy's net worth in another one of his big paws. "Autumn comes in for breakfast after her morning run."

"How will I know her?"

He laughed. "Endurance is a small town. Word spreads fast when a newcomer stays in town. She knows you're here."

"Really?"

"Don't worry. Autumn will help out if it's too much for you to handle."

Ivy gave him a coy smile. "You'd be surprised how much I can handle."

Before he took her in his arms and tested her limits, Owen raised his hand in farewell. Maybe, the drive would cool his jets.

As if an afterthought, Ivy called out, "Don't go through my things."

He didn't reply. He strode out the back door, grass and gravel crunching under his work boots. Cai climbed into the Wrangler's back seat, and he buckled him in, checking the harness's security.

"Owen Tate," he heard Ivy's soprano above the distinctive rumble of the V-8 engine. "I'm serious."

He chuckled. "Nothing's off limits in my house, my bar, or on my employee. I have the right to search, sweetheart," he called back.

Backing out of the yard, he paused when he saw her standing on the porch, hands on those hips. The woman sure could fill out a pair of jeans. The breeze pinned that tie-dye shirt to her curves. Owen's grip tightened on the wheel. Heaven help him, Ivy tempted him beyond reason.

"Not everything around here belongs to you," she laughed.

Ain't that the truth of it. Owen hoped he remembered that he had dominion over everything that happened in his bar. He had no rights to Ivy. Nope, he belonged with his son and the memory of his wife. Now if he could just convince his body that Ivy Summers was just a temporary infatuation, the lonely yearning of a single man.

"Forget about your pack. Take a look at the menu. Get breakfast started, Ivy. Luke and Hank will be here in a minute."

She had to assume he would snoop through her pack. In reality, Owen hadn't made a decision one way or the other. He just didn't want her to leave while he was gone, that's all. Having to have the last word, Ivy yelled as he rounded the corner onto Miller Road.

"Don't go tucking my unmentionables in your pocket for later."

Instead of responding, Owen popped the truck in gear. Head hanging out the window, he said. "Open up the bar. Customers will want a hot breakfast and plenty of coffee. My number is on the fridge."

It was unfair, but he smiled at the thought of her being home when he returned.

CHAPTER THREE

I vy released a shuddered breath when Owen and his tough guy truck disappeared from sight. Wow, one hundred dollars plus the forty hidden in her bra would buy her a bus ticket far away from this town, and especially the owner of No Limit. The man had entirely too much sexy for one 'Y' chromosome. When she'd entered the kitchen and saw him taking care of his son, making breakfast, the sight had been a balm to a very old, very deep sore spot in her heart. What would it have felt like to have had a father like that when she was growing up? Her mother had barely kept a roof over their heads and food on the table.

The veritable parade of men Ivy had been forced to call uncles took more from Crystal Summers than they gave. Ivy closed her eyes against the painful memories: the hunger, the fights, and the bruises her mother bore. As soon as she'd turned eighteen, she'd left home with the first man who'd claimed to love her.

Dean had cared for her in his own way. Problem was, he adored his casino visits a lot more. It had taken about six weeks for Ivy to discover her prince charming had a healthy gambling habit that ate up the money they earned at an all-night diner on the Biloxi coast.

Shortly thereafter, Dean's undying love morphed into scathing criticism. He never hit her, not with his fist, anyway. His berating rants were painful enough. One morning he'd stumbled in drunk and broke, having gambled away his earnings at one of the many casinos. Ivy left him in the rundown motel on the outskirts to Biloxi, Mississippi hours later.

After Dean, she'd tied herself to Trevor, a drummer in a Rhythm & Blues band headed for Louisiana in a VW camper. Endless booze, easy women, and Ecstasy gave her a short shelf-life with Trevor, since she engaged in none of the above. Johnny and his bike came along when money was short and her options shorter.

A few times she'd considered using the precious minutes on her prepaid phone to call the Second Chance House hotline. She'd gotten close to one of the volunteers there, Lina James. Lina worked as a psych nurse at Shell Cove Medical Center. After a few weeks of steady visits, the caregiver had grown on Ivy. Funny, right? She was the one in the women's shelter, yet she didn't accept help readily. But, Ivy trusted Lina enough to accept her personal cell number. If ever in trouble, she made Ivy promise to call her.

More than once, Ivy had dialed the number, but decided a successful woman with a career and all that education didn't really want someone like her hanging around.

Bang. Bang.

She jerked at the thump on the countertop. Owen had been right. By the time she ran upstairs, changed her clothes, and hot-footed it back to the kitchen, Hank Stewart and Luke Cole were chomping at the bit for a hot meal. Both men had shared their personal dossiers as if she were an old friend coming home after a long absence. She enjoyed the camaraderie. The conversation, jovial and light, earned both men a spot on Ivy's friend roster.

"Hey, pretty woman. I need my breakfast."

Seemed Owen's customers shared the owner's personality. It seemed bossy and demanding men chose to eat their breakfast in bars. Seriously, who came to a bar and grille for breakfast? Other single dads like Owen, she surmised.

"I'm coming," she said grabbing two plated meals of scrambled eggs, sausage, and toast, "hold your mule, Hank."

Yeah, she was quick with names. Hank and Luke worked at the University of California Endurance Facilities plant about twenty miles north of town. She learned the guys were single dads, too. Hank had a ten-year-old son named Elliot who loved to fish. And, Luke's daughter, Shiloh, would start kindergarten in the fall.

Leaning over the bar, Ivy sat hot plates with steam still rising from the eggs in front of both men. She smiled as they ate with gusto. According to the gossip, Owen had the cheapest prices in all of Placer County.

"Hmm," Hank said, sniffing his food. "You a darn good cook, pretty woman," he winked. "You and Owen dating, yet?"

The compliment warmed Ivy's heart, the insinuation did not. Ivy laughed off the inquiry. "I got here last night."

With a good-natured laugh, Hank gave her a wink. "Endurance is a small town, Ivy. Not many women in these parts," he grinned. "Especially none as pretty as you. Just thought with you spending the night and cooking this morning, that Owen had tagged you before the other fellas could."

Owen had tagged her all right, but it wasn't his cooking that she was hungry for. Growing up in a single-parent household, she learned to cook for herself before she could read. Well, that wasn't a fair assessment. With her Dyslexia, she still struggled with more complex books. Daily practice helped. During their frequent stays at the women's shelters, she committed as many books, magazines, and newspapers as she could to her mental library. Even though she didn't have much education, she valued lifelong learning.

"Thank you and the name's Ivy Summers, not pretty woman, cowboy."

Luke grinned up at her, his boyish smile dazzling in the bright rays pouring in through the windows.

"Pretty name for a pretty lady." He tipped his ball cap on his head causing a few dark brown strands to peak up. "You want to go out with me tonight?"

Ivy was used to men flirting with her. With her life on the road, she used whatever she could to an advantage. A soft smile and a listening ear went a long way for a girl without much education, transportation, or money.

"Sorry," she shrugged, "gotta work."

Ivy new the game. Always let a man think he had a chance, and he'd keep in pursuit.

"What about Fri-,"

The bell over the door clattered.

"Duty calls," she said blowing Hank a kiss.

When Owen left with Cai, Ivy had changed into more appropriate work attire. A cut off tie-dye tank top and a mini skirt...and never the two shall meet. A little midriff and her favorite black combat boots completed the look. For the hair, she'd undid her two-strand twists and pulled her natural curls into a messy ponytail. For whatever reason, men seemed to like the untamed schoolgirl look. Just like the two at the counter, the three new guys entering No Limit wore plaid shirts, faded denim jeans, and college-football caps with bills that hid their eyes.

"Excuse me, fellas," she said to Hank and Luke. "Let me get the new guys settled at a table."

One the new guys, the older of the three drawled. "No need, little lady. We'll come to you."

Ivy smiled. "Well, aren't you generous, this morning."

When all three smiled back, Ivy could see her tip meter inching in a very lucrative direction.

"Name's Fenley Willis. These here," he pointed to the two younger men, "are my boys, Kent and Nolan. Raised them myself, right here in Endurance, after breast cancer claimed my wife. Both of them is marrying age...if you're interested." He grinned. "So am I, if you don't mind a little gray in your coffee."

Ivy laughed, and the bar erupted in laughter right along with her. This new job might just work out.

"Well now, I'll have to put on you the list behind Luke."

Hank refusing to be left out added, "Don't forget about me, Ivy. I met you first."

She looked down the bar into dark brown eyes, light with neighborly fun. "I think Owen holds that title," she challenged.

"Yeah," he called back, "but, O's a grump since our high school days." So, Hank and Owen were the same age. An idea came to her. She was more than capable of doing a little snooping, too.

Taking the bar towel from her shoulder, she mimicked a pop to his fanny. "Hey, you're too old to be name calling. Besides, that grump signs my check."

"Twenty-nine is not old," he frowned, "unless you're into that type of thing."

He wiggled his brows and all five men released a cacophony of uproarious laughs. The ribbing done, Ivy turned her attention back to Fenley.

"So, what can I get you three handsome bachelors for breakfast?" Familiar with the menu, the group ordered the breakfast. Thanks to Owen's hurried instruction, she'd cooked enough sausage and bacon for several customers. The eggs and toast, she'd made to order.

Ting-a-ling. Ting-a-ling. Once again, the door opened.

A fourth man walked in. While the other men wore denim and boots, this dark-haired man with a matching beard wore a dress shirt and slacks. He had a quiet intelligence about him, but he smiled and Ivy returned the greeting.

"That's Rui Conners," Fenley whispered, without her asking. These men were virtual wellsprings of information.

One of the Fenley's sons waved. It was Nolan the taller of the two. "He's a professor at the university."

Luke chimed in, changing the subject. "Ivy, you didn't call me handsome."

Turning in his direction, she pushed her lips into a subtle pout. "That's because it goes without saying, cutie."

Hank chucked him in the arm. "Stop fishing for compliments."

While the men carried on in a playful banter, she disappeared to the kitchen to fill their orders.

With The Willis' eating, and the others pulling a Hoover vacuum maneuver over the last crumbs, Ivy focused on the professor pretending to peruse the one sheet menu. He was looking for someone. Who, she wondered. Maybe, the professor and Delaney were an item?

Ivy approached the man, deciding he would be the best person to talk with about free online classes. She'd taken a couple through the years. While at the Second Chance House, the counselors had advocated higher education. The online format removed the pitying looks and judgment that haunted a lot of the women and girls they provided services for.

"I'm Ivy," she said by way of introduction. "Heard you were a teacher at the college." She slid into the booth across from him. A stricken expression crossed his face as his eyes darted around the room.

"Yes, yes...I am," he stammered.

High color, varying shades of red, had infused his cheeks. Handsome, but the shy type. Not a quality the men in Ivy's life possessed. Johnny had been charismatic and funny, with a Brad Pitt smile. His brother, Poe, ... well Poe had been the polar opposite.

"Can we talk later, about some possible free online adult education classes offered by your college?"

Professor Conners looked ready to bolt. He dropped his eyes to her cleavage and frowned. Men didn't frown at her *tatas*. If fact, when the bell chimed a new arrival, he scrambled to his feet.

"There's an enrollment process. I'll give you the number of someone who can help you."

The man disappeared faster than a genie in a bottle. Looking down at her exposed flesh, Ivy thought to maybe turn it down a notch. This crowd seemed to be happy with friendly conversation and a smile. Yes, she'd change as soon as—

"What the Sam Adams are you wearing?"

Ivy jumped at Owen's now familiar bellow. Wiggling out of the booth to stand to her feet, she faced off her new boss. His jaw, though chiseled, appeared to be cut from marble. His blue eyes were hard, piercing, and fixed on her.

"Now, Owen just calm-" a male voice interjected.

"Shut up, Luke," he growled.

Straightening her spine, Ivy refused to cower. "You're back," she smiled, walking toward him. "I was just about to close out Luke and Hank's orders," she said pointing to the men peering at the interaction between her and a very pissed off male. "Now, you can do it," she snapped.

"In the back, Ivy." When she didn't move. He roared. "Now."

Luke rose to his feet, leaving the bar stool, spinning on its base. Ivy raised a hand to stop him.

"Don't," she ordered. "I can handle Owen." That seemed to bring a bright smile to his handsome face.

"I believe you can, Ivy."

Owen gave Luke an incredulous look before storming off. His boots pounding the floor like a stampede of wild mustangs.

When Ivy entered the kitchens, Owen had his back to her, gazing out the window.

"You wanted to see me, boss?"

Like a predator in wait, he spun and stalked toward her.

"I see too much of you," he ground out through tight lips. That fire from last night was back in his eyes and she wondered what really had lit his fuse.

"You outraged on behalf of your customer's moral fiber?"

He met her eyes, but not before glancing down at her body. "Something like that."

"They're all big boys, Owen."

He narrowed his eyes. "Bigger after seeing you dressed like that."

"Jealous?"

"Let's just say I don't like other men looking at you."

"Looking isn't touching, Owen." Why was she digging a rabbit hole? She felt the pull of attraction between them. Drawing attention to that fact would only work against her. Ivy didn't need or want any attachments.

He closed the space between them. "Looking leads to touching."

Don't take the bait, Ivy. Stop talking.

"You like looking at me, Owen Tate," she whispered, totally swallowing the worm, the hook, and probably a good bit of the line.

"I do," he admitted. "I'll love touching you more."

Oh, the promise in those words. Is this what she'd been pushing for? A small part of Ivy wanted Owen to say the words. He wanted her.

She should have changed back into her jeans before he returned home. Wait. Why was she considering changing for him? No way would she make that mistake again. Hadn't she and her mother performed for the endless men's parade...the hair, the makeup, and the dresses. Nausea rolled at the image of her in a dress. She hadn't worn one since that day.

"Hey, you okay?"

Owen stood in front her now, concern having banked the fire in his eyes. But, his body heat stoked her from the top of her head down to her pinky toes. Wow, he confused her. Cold one second, raging inferno the next.

"Of course," she said, shaking off the effect of his soothing tone. Ivy realized she had to appear to bend to get what she needed in life. However, she would not transform herself for him. Not for anyone. She was her only meal ticket. She could only depend on herself. Owen Tate and this job was a means to an end. Focus, Ivy.

"There's a dress code?"

His eye flashed with irritation. Hey, why let him hold her to a standard he failed to establish?

"You know there isn't."

"So, what's the problem, boss?"

He growled. "Problem. The problem, sweetheart, is your tight little body is going to cause a riot."

She gave him a smirk. Though, the fact that he found her body appealing meant she was sexy, right?

"Has it happened in the past?"

Faster than she could process it, he had her in his arms, his hard body pressed into her softening curves.

"Ivy," he growled. The hunger in the way he said her name had her knees buckling. If he didn't have her anchored to him, she would have surely melted onto the floor. He pressed his lips to her forehead. His breathing was choppy and seemed as if she could hear the pounding of his heartbeat in her head. "Go upstairs and change."

Her breath came in rapid exhalations and an ache started to build low and deep inside. What was happening to her? She couldn't let him gain the upper hand. A man like Owen Tate took charge. Ivy knew the wrong man could easily ensnare an unsuspecting woman. And, regardless of how gentle and caring Owen Tate was with his son, he was the wrong kind of man for her.

"No," she said in a breathy reply.

He pulled her in closer, his warm breath caressing the curve of her ear. Liking the feel of him, she angled her head wanting him closer. Then she felt him. Not just his generous muscles, but the hard length of him. She gasped.

"Yeah," he grunted.

He dropped his head to her neck, inhaling. "Go change, Ivy. If one of them touches you..." he trailed off. "Trust these words, sweetheart. I will riot."

He would what? She jerked back.

"But—," How could this be? He didn't know her and now he wanted to pull this barbarian routine?

A heavy hand landed on her backside. The sting traveled liked a firehouse's alarm straight to her center. Heat blossomed at the heart of her.

"Ouch," she yelped.

He chuckled. "There's more where that came from." Squeezing her waist, he said, "Get upstairs, sweetheart. Come back with your arms, legs, and middle covered."

She narrowed her eyes, ready to protest.

"Test me, Ivy. My palm could use the workout."

Her eyes widened in shock. "You wouldn't?"

Desire crept into his gaze and her insides quivered. Owen Tate would paddle her backside and enjoy it. Scary truth, Ivy believed she might like it.

IVY Summers was the worst kind of temptation. How the heck was Owen going to keep his hands off of her? Maybe, he should tell her the job was over. He could load her and that ratty backpack in the truck. It would take less than two hours to drop her off in Sacramento with a bus ticket.

He stormed out of the kitchen with three breakfast plates. Fenley, Kent, and Nolan stared down at the usual he fed them every morning. Owen frowned when the three men kept their eyes peeled to the closed kitchen door.

"What?" Owen snapped.

"Where's Ivy?" Kent asked.

Kent was the youngest of Fenley's boys. If memory served, Kent would be old enough for a beer this year. Either way, he was too young to be asking after Ivy.

"Why?" Owen snarled.

Fenley spoke first. "'Cause looking at her will make this burnt crap you cooked taste better."

Owen sat down three mugs, filling each with dark roasted brew. He slammed each cup in front of a plate.

"Never complained about my cooking before."

Fenley rubbed a hand behind his neck. "That's before we saw what Luke and Hank got."

Hank stood and patted his belly. "Yep, Ivy took good care of us. Seems to me the early bird gets the cute waitress."

Nolan stood and leaned over the counter. "Hey, what's taking Ivy so long, anyway?"

"She's fine," Owen roared.

Understatement of the decade. Did they think he'd murdered the woman? He'd be more likely to kiss her senseless before dragging her into his bed for the next five days. Why did she keep talking about leaving? Ivy Summers gave breathtaking a new definition. Warm peach cobbler with real vanilla bean ice cream, that's what she reminded Owen of. Warm, sweet, and sinfully delicious.

"Ah hmmm," Fenley said, stroking his chin, "then why come she's not out here?"

"Yeah," Kent joined in. "Send Delaney back, too."

"She's not here today." Owen grimaced, remembering he'd have to address the Delaney issue.

"Oh, I saw-,"

With a fierce scowl, he silenced the young peanut gallery.

Crossing his arms over his chest, Owen smirked at Fenley. "Don't like my company?"

The crusty old viticulturist chuckled. "Never have. You're kid's cute, though."

Willis Vineyard was one of the largest grape plantations in the county. As a fifth-generation vintner, he was well respected in the region.

Ivy came bouncing through the door. She'd lost the miniskirt for a pair of jeans so tight *his* baby makers hurt. The long sleeve shirt, had rips that started under her breasts and continued to her abdomen. He didn't know how it was possible, but the woman looked even sexier with the added material.

"Hot grease in the skillet," someone muttered.

Hank took a swallow of his juice. "Luke, let's drive the twenty miles back for lunch."

Ivy gave them a welcoming smile. "I'll be here fellas. We're having baked chicken and oven-roasted sweet potatoes for lunch."

Owen listened in amazement. His lunch menu consisted of cold sandwiches, hot dogs, hamburgers and fries.

Hank and Luke finished up their breakfast. Owen could see fifteen dollars between the two empty plates. He charged five dollars for a hot breakfast plate. The guys had left too much money. He took two steps and picked up the extra five.

"Put us down for two plates, Ivy." Hank winked. "And the five is for you, doll face."

Owen watched as Ivy lit up like Hank had given her the keys to a brand-new Tesla.

"You guys are the best," she beamed. "See you at noon."

What in the green hell? Owen frowned. She was working over his customers. His sweet little doll face was a first-class hustler.

The bell over the door clamored as the two men exited. When he heard one of them say Ivy's name in an appreciative tone, his gut clenched.

Distracted by his own anger, he damn near saw red when Ivy patted Fenley's hand and the smiling idiot handed her a twenty-dollar bill.

"Keep the change, Ivy." He glared at Owen. "The boys and I want you to serve us for lunch."

Not one of his regular customers left regular tips for breakfast. It was the reason he only asked Delaney to cover the morning crowd. There wasn't enough dough on the back end for her if a second waitress worked the floor, too.

Ivy made quick work of removing the dishes and wiping down the counter.

"The people around here are friendly."

The comment, aimed into the atmosphere more than to him only, twerked his annoyance higher.

"Ivy."

She walked over to him, eyes unflinching.

"Yes, Owen?"

Her voice was soft and seductive. Dang. An image of her screaming his name as he got lost inside her cut through his mind. What was he angry about again? Honest to goodness, the woman with her untamed scent and sienna smooth skin scrambled his brain. He swallowed. She angled her head, watching him. Her hair, piled in a loose ponytail, moved with her. Sexy. Owen frowned. When had ponytails started looking sexy to him? His attraction to Ivy Summers was making him nuts.

"Lunch crowd starts before noon," he said pushing past her. He needed to put some distance between them before he did something really dumb, like take her to his bed.

She licked her bottom lip, and then exhaled. "Okay. I'll be ready."

That's what he was afraid of.

CHAPTER FOUR

Ivy stirred the bubbling brown sugar, nutmeg, and cinnamon in a skillet. The churning in her belly stopped the minute Owen left to pick up Cai from school. Owen had stuck too close after the last of the breakfast crowd dissipated. He'd unloaded crates and boxes until sweat drenched his torso. Truth be told, Ivy had singed her fingers more than once when he removed his shirt. She'd looked, taken a mental picture, and then smiled to herself. That bad boy would be on rewind for the rest of the day. Ivy thanked the cosmos when Owen said he had to leave.

Surprisingly, surveying the storage shelves she found everything she needed to make lunch. Owen was well-organized. He had a computerized inventory system and all the shelves in the stock room were labeled. Ivy had worked at a variety of jobs during her travels from Florida to California. Hands down, Owen Tate had a business mind and the bar was well run.

The tension between them had to stop. Nothing good would come of a liaison. In fact, the closer he hovered the more she knew she needed to leave, sooner rather than later. She planned to tell him tonight. If Delaney returned in the morning, Ivy would take her pay and vamoose. Ivy never doubted that she'd find a way to take care of herself, but a man with a child needed a woman that could help him. With her barely-graduated high school education and sporadic job history, Ivy had nothing to offer a ready-made family. Though she had no doubt that sharing Owen's bed would be like fireworks at Disney World, but sleeping with him would be a mistake. Owen Tate was not the leaving kind...she was.

The back door opened. Cai came running inside. A blur of messy blonde hair, mouth ringed in chocolate milk, and little grubby hands filled with papers.

"Ivy," he sang, arms outstretched as he ran straight for her.

"Smells good in here," Owen said.

That had been her goal. Her mother had taught her that a man's brain started in his nose. *Get your scents right Ivy and you'll have him eating out of your hand.* Ivy remembered those hands covered in blood. The ambulance. The gurney. The low hum of a flatline.

Stopping at the stove, she turned the handles in, before dropping low. Cai threw both arms around her neck and hugged her. Closing her eyes, she inhaled his innocence, and squeezed him back.

"Hey, baby boy." She smiled, releasing him.

"I missed you." He smiled up at her and Ivy's heart overflowed with happiness.

What should she say? She looked up to find Owen watching them. Her boss hung back by the door, his long frame leaning in the opening.

"Well, I thought about you, too."

His eyes stretched in disbelief, but she could see her statement made him happy.

"Really?"

"Oh yeah," she said, nodding her head. "Check out the table. I made those just for you."

Quickly, he wiggled the Ironman backpack off his tiny shoulders and ran to the table. Ivy wondered if her mother's advice applied to little boys.

At the center of the table he spied the sweet potato muffins piled high on a platter. Cai began to jump up and down. Owen moved closer.

"Daddy, daddy. Ivy made me cupcakes."

An expression appeared on Owen's face. Before she could discern the meaning, it disappeared.

"Did she now?"

"Go on, Cai. You can eat one," Ivy encouraged. Like a good boy, he looked to his father.

"We'll both will try one," Owen said.

Long legs narrowed the distance between them. Scooping Cai up into his arms, Owen picked up one of the still-warm muffins. He offered Cai the first bite, and then the brute tossed the rest of the muffin in his mouth.

"Whoa," he said, his eyes stretched wide in shock. "These are crazy delicious."

She laughed, heart light with joy. It was nice to see him smile. Ivy had the suspicion it didn't happen often. "Glad you like them," she announced with a flourish and a bow.

Cai laughed, causing a little orange fluff to join the chocolate stains around his mouth.

"I'm driving you to Cherron's in the morning. These babies need to be on the menu."

"Yummy," Cai said, mouth still full. "Can I have my own cupcake, daddy?"

"Who's Cherron?"

A lot of names were tossed around this morning. There was Ma Hildie's Grocers and Trina's Treasures if she needed clothes. A woman named Amelie worked in the museum Ivy spotted on the walk into Endurance. Ivy remembered the sign said something about a library being inside the museum, too.

"Cherron is the town baker. She's owns the Cupcakery."

If he thought her muffins could hold a candle to anything a professional baker made, he really meant the compliment as sincere. Compliments were few in Ivy's acquaintances.

"I can walk you know."

Owen's face darkened for a second. His expression closed. "I don't want you walking," he rasped. "I'll take you in the truck."

Something is his expression had Ivy nodding her agreement.

To Cai he said, "Just one more, buddy."

Ivy smiled at the sullen frown that Cai aimed at his father. Owen didn't budge, not that she expected him to.

Owen gave him that love father's reserved just for their offspring. "There's dinner in a little bit."

She, of course, was a noodle for the kid. She would have let him eat the whole platter and ruined him for dinner. Again, her silly heart did a little flip in her chest. Owen Tate's love for his son was evident. Loving parents set limits and provided direction. Her mother stopped giving her any advice after the fifth shelter stay. Ivy had to rely on her own wits. And, they screamed it was time to go. She didn't need any attachments. Owen Tate and his son would stick like peanut butter on toast.

"Yes, Daddy."

Grabbing his muffin, Cai asked if he could eat in front of the television. Owen nodded in agreement.

"Thank you for my cupcakes, Ivy. They're...they are good."

"You're very welcome, baby. I'm glad you like them," she said smoothing his hair down.

Once again, she and Owen were alone. That tingle started beneath her skin.

"You didn't have to do that." Owen circled her before coming to stand in front of her.

Ivy ran a nervous hand over her lip. "It was no problem."

Reaching for her hand, Owen captured her trembling fingers in his. "Didn't say it was a problem."

She licked her lip. What did he want her to say? As if he'd heard the thought.

He asked, "Why did you do it?"

She shrugged. "I was already cooking, so...." She let her words trail off.

"So," he said, rubbing her knuckles with his thumb. "You surprised my son."

Why had she thought to do something for Cai? Why couldn't Owen just drop it? She baked. It was no big deal. If she had her own kitchen, she'd cook all the time. It relaxed her.

"I kind of owe him."

A slow smile covered Owen's full lips. "You owe, Cai? How?"

"I...." She heard the nervous shudder to the one syllable word. "I, ah...turned off the light in the bathroom last night. Could have been a mess for the little guy."

Owen chuckled and stepped closer. "I gave you a job."

She swallowed. "And?"

He lowered his head. His lips were so close to hers, they shared the same breath. "Do you want to give me something, too?"

Well now, why hadn't she thought of that? Because, during his absence she'd been trying to convince herself to go upstairs, roll up her clothes, and get the heck out of Endurance before Owen got back.

"Owen," she breathed. Tell him, Ivy. "When Delaney comes back tomorrow. I'll be moving on."

Owen's sharp inhale shocked her. His hand tightened on hers. Something in his blue eyes slammed shut, but not before she saw the pain. Had she hurt him?

"Daddy."

At the sound of small feet padding into the kitchen, Ivy jumped. Everything was happening too fast. Why would her leaving upset Owen? Forgetting, the hot stove was at her back, she stumbled backwards. Oh God, how bad would she burn herself. All of a sudden, a steel band circled her waist, stopping her momentum faster than a solid wall. Owen's arm was around her, hard, strong, and safe. She exhaled in relief.

"Yes, son."

"Can I invite Ivy to my birthday party on Saturday?"

Owen looked down, locking eyes with hers.

"Yes, you can."

His voiced was filled with something far more dangerous than a five-year old's party. Ivy couldn't look away, couldn't break the spell he had her under.

"Ivy," Cai called out.

"Yes, baby?" Ivy said, not breaking eye contact with the man who held her.

"Will you come to my birthday party?"

This was a mistake. It was Monday. How could she resist Owen Tate if she stayed under his roof for another five days? Already, her body craved his touch. The arm around her waist tightened.

"I'll stay," she whispered, never looking away from Owen's formidable gaze.

Ivy expected the arm supporting her to relax, nope. If anything, his hold became more secure.

"Yippie. Can you make my birthday cake?"

Cai chattered on about party hats, miniature golf, and classmates.

"Of course I will, baby."

Owen's gaze softened with gratitude, but Ivy recognized something in his eyes she hadn't seen in a long time —possession. Oh, those sweet potato muffins had gotten her in a serious pickle.

CHAPTER FIVE

Owen smirked at No Limit's packed tables. Word spread fast in a small town. Seemed everyone had gotten word of his new menu and more importantly, his new waitress. More than half the crowd were single men from town. All twelve bar stools were turned away from the bar, facing the dining area, with the men watching Ivy. Fenley, Kent, and Nolan were back. Sappy idiots. They wouldn't let her leave any more than he would.

Approaching the booth closest to the door, he deposited two glasses of chardonnay hooked between the fingers of one hand in front of two brunettes dressed in tight blouses and loose smiles. They would probably leave with a couple of cowboys on their arm. Headed back to the bar, he noticed Luke and Hank had snuck in seats at the bar.

Ivy was in high-wattage mode, laughing and smiling like everyone she came in contact with was a long-lost friend. Owen threw a damp dish towel over his shoulder and headed in her direction. Did the woman own a stitch of clothing that didn't raise a man's blood pressure? She still wore the combat boots, which for her seemed totally appropriate.

Tonight's tie-dye t-shirt had twin swirls in bright red, orange, and blue that merged at the gentle valley between her mounds. Now, why did he bite his lip at the image of him kissing her there?

Owen was just about to reach her when Autumn Raine, the babysitter, called his name. Stopping, he waited for Autumn to approach. At twenty-six, Autumn was only three years younger than him, but she seemed more settled.

He glanced in Ivy's direction only to find she'd vacated the spot in front of Abel Burney and his date, Julie. Doing a quick scan, he found her at one of the corner booths near the front of the bar talking with a table full of guys he'd seen a few times since the start of tourist season. Owen recognized the type. Playboys with more than enough money to dabble in the races, the women, and the recreational marijuana that flowed in and out of Endurance.

Owen loved his town, but he wasn't naive to the seedier vices of small town living. Bored kids with money could find themselves in a heap of trouble if their parents failed to remain vigilant. Hence, the reason he hired Autumn to keep Cai upstairs during peak business hours.

"What's up, Autumn?"

Tonight, Autumn chose to leave her afro-textured hair loose. A full halo, thick with dark auburn curls framed her face. The woman rarely wore makeup allowing her flawless golden skin to serve as an unmarked canvas. Her body and face caught and held a man's attention, but for some reason there wasn't a grain of attraction between them.

"Wondered if I could cut out an hour early? There's a new band playing at Diego's tonight."

As a music therapy major, Autumn took every opportunity to support the local artists as well as the variety of guest musicians traveling through the town's only live music venue.

"Sure thing," he said.

Thinking their conversation over, he turned to leave.

"Owen, who's the new girl?"

"Her name's Ivy."

Autumn waited for him to say more. Owen found he didn't want to say too much about Ivy. He felt protective of her. If she wanted Autumn to know more, then he was sure Ivy could do her own talking.

"Hmmm," came Autumn's soft reply. Again, Owen turned to walk away when he heard Autumn say, "Cai said she stayed the night."

Dag nab it. He needed to have a talk with Cai, the little chatterbox. His son had divulged enough information for one day, first the bar-b-q toast with Ivy this morning, and now about their overnight guest with Autumn.

Autumn's brown eyes, as warm and welcoming as her name, flashed with concern. Owen grimaced. In all the months he'd known her, their friendship had been transparent. No doubt, she questioned what Ivy's arrival signaled in his life. Heck if Owen knew. From the moment she'd sat at his table, he knew he wanted her. Why that was so, he refused to question his inner workings. There was nothing wrong with a grown man enjoying the company of a full-grown, sexy-as-a-late-night-storm woman.

"She did," he confirmed. Immediately, his brain took him back to Ivy standing in his hallway wearing one of her t-shirts, her legs bare. His blood heated. He tried to keep his body re-laxed but failed. Autumn's audible gasp sounded, and he knew.

She stared at him in shock. Was his attraction to the little spitfire obvious?

"Oh no," she breathed. "Owen, how?"

The answer was yes. This time he welcomed the tension that consumed his body.

"Don't worry. She'll be gone soon."

If possible, Autumn's expression became more grave.

"That's makes me worry more. You can't keep your eyes off of her."

Owen straightened his spine, not liking the implications. "I can handle Ivy Summers."

No sooner than the words had left his mouth, loud voices, mostly male started to climb in the far corner of the bar.

Assuming a few of the guys had consumed one beer too many, he didn't immediately respond. Most of the locals liked to egg one another on, but the bluster usually piped down before fists started to flow. Owen prided himself on running a drama-free establishment. The cowboys saved the fisticuffs for the streets, not his bar.

Something drew Autumn's attention. When her mouth dropped open, Owen followed her line of sight, and his lungs seized, seconds before a roar built in the back of his throat.

"Put me down," his woman screeched.

Ivy's panicked voice cut away the noise in the room. His heart thumped against his rib cage. Who dared to put a hand on his Ivy? Yes, his Ivy. She was his responsibility to protect.

Red crowded his vision.

That was the only word to describe the rage boiling in his veins when he saw Ivy tossed over one of the customer's shoulders. He advanced on his patrons like a charging bull. The crowd split faster than the Red Sea, and Owen was ready to rain down an unholy terror on the man who'd touched her.

Owen got to the center of the crowd, just as some buffed up meathead with overlong blonde dreadlocks and a scruffy beard whirled Ivy around in his arms.

"Stop it, you nut tart," Ivy bellowed at the top of her lungs.

Owen didn't recognize any of the men at the table. The thing about a small town was strangers stuck out like a priest at the racetrack. And the man holding Ivy, would be considered a stud. The guy probably was used to intimidating others based on his size alone. Owen grew up in these mountains. Boys learned early in life to defend themselves against all threats, four-legged and two. He could bench press twice his weight and pissing him off added another seventy-pounds to that number.

"Put her down," Owen growled.

"Dude—,"

That was the only word he got out before Owen snatched Ivy from his arms and tucked her into his side.

"You okay, sweetheart?"

Though Ivy held a brave face, he felt the tremors in her limbs.

She nodded but remained silent. He'd pound this—what had she called him, nut tart into the ground. Owen curled the fingers on his right hand into a fist.

"All of you," he said, letting pure menace and brutal intent enter his voice. "Get out. Don't come back."

Blondie looked to his friends, who watched the confrontation with eager eyes.

"Look, dude," he grinned. "We were just having a bit of fun, with little Ivy."

She stiffened at the suggestive tone lacing his voice. His buddies still occupying the booth chuckled. Owen pulled her in closer to his warmth, using his body as comfort.

"Time's up."

Rearing back his fist, Owen delivered one punch to the pretty boy's chin and the heavyweight dropped faster than a soufflé. When blondie's friends saw he was out like a blown lightbulb, Owen gave a second warning.

"Who's next?"

All of a sudden, the booth cleared like roaches under bright lights. Two of the silent partners scooped up Blondie on the way out. Raging bull mad, Owen wanted to go after each one of them. Ivy must have felt his muscles coil in anticipation.

"I'm safe, Owen. Stay here with me."

Yeah, he reminded himself. Ivy was safe in his arms. He pulled her in close, dropping a kiss to her fragrant curls. Man, he was a goner.

IVY swallowed the lump in her throat, still unsure how the dreadlocked nut tart had gotten his hands on her. Usually she was so careful when in the company of men. Sure, she flirted but she didn't do laps, pats, or rubs.

Everything about Owen Tate and his charming body had her off her game. Her mother would have been disappointed that Ivy had brought trouble to her man. Because of her carelessness, Owen had hit a man. A woman should make life easier for her man, she could hear her mom's words. For all her mom's lessons, Crystal Summers had spent her life dependent on a man for her worth, her next meal, and a roof over her head.

She'd watched from the corner of her eye while Owen stood over by the bar talking to another woman. Ivy had struggled to keep her smile from slipping. So, he enjoyed the company of more than one female, she'd thought. She should have known he was too good to be true. Again, she blamed those darn sweet potato muffins. Next time, she'd keep the baked goodies to herself.

"Ivy." Owen's large finger glided under her chin and lifted. "Are you hurt?"

They had entered the kitchen. Ivy lifted herself up on both forearms and deposited her bottom on the smooth countertop. Luke and Hank had taken over getting the regulars back in their seats.

"I should get back out there," she said sliding to her feet to stand in front of him.

He stopped her. He circled her waist and placed her back on the counter. "Answer my question."

Why did he have to investigate everything?

She tried to sidestep away. "I'm fine," she huffed. "I should go check on the floor."

"Something's bothering you beyond those yahoos," he challenged, not letting the subject drop. "And Autumn will take care of the bar."

The woman who'd been talking with Owen had grabbed a tray and started serving customers before he'd taken Ivy out of the dining area. Amazingly, Owen seemed real comfortable with her jumping right in and taking over. He'd lost his wife two years ago. Had Autumn fulfilled the desires Owen obviously had?

The mention of the other woman reminded Ivy how much it bothered her to see Owen with another woman. True, he only offered her a job out of necessity, but a spark existed between them. It upset her see evidence of another woman in his life.

"I don't need you to coddle me, Owen Tate. I can take care of myself," she snapped.

"Never implied you couldn't, but a man takes care of his woman."

His woman?

"Isn't Autumn the babysitter?" she asked.

He narrowed his eyes on her. "She works here sometimes too."

Well, that was vague. Ivy worked at No Limit sometimes too, yet Owen had no problem touching her at every opportunity. Did he share the same type of relationship with the cute redhead?

"Below or above stairs?" she demanded, holding his gaze.

He frowned. "Both."

Ivy's heart plummeted into her boots. So, he admitted there was something between him and Autumn. She shook off his hold.

"I'm fine," she said, hopping off the kitchen counter where he'd placed her.

Before she could take one step, he had an arm around her waist.

"Don't think so."

Gripping his massive forearm, she pushed. He didn't budge.

"Let go, Owen."

With one arm he lifted her off the ground. Ivy yelped.

"Hey," she protested.

His strength fascinated her. Never had a man come to her rescue with such brute force, and then touch her with such tenderness.

"Explain yourself."

He was the one that needed to explain. How could he tease her, and then bring the other woman in her face? Ivy made no qualms about capitalizing on her every advantage, but she didn't do love triangles. Her heart fluttered at the word love. It would be easy to fall for a man like Owen, if he were faithful. Autumn dashed that hope.

"Look you're hot, Owen. There's enough hormone juice flowing between us, I could bottle the stuff, but," she paused, "I can't get mixed up with you and Autumn."

Owen studied her for a moment, eyes hard. Then, to her surprise, he started to laugh. His body shook with the effort. Now, he found her feelings humorous?

"Ivy," he smiled, wiping at his eyes. "Autumn is strictly Cai's babysitter."

Her mouth dropped open, stunned. She felt a warm heat infuse her cheeks. "Seriously? I'm pretty good at reading people. You two were in a heated conversation."

He placed her in front of him, pinning her body between his broad chest and the counter.

He twerked her nose with his index finger. "We talked about you."

"Yes," he continued. "Autumn's concerned about this hormone flow between us, too."

Crossing her arms over her chest, Ivy narrowed her eyes. "Cai's babysitter is considerate," she said with mock appreciation.

Owen's blue eyes sparkled with new awareness. "You're jealous."

Bet his tight butt, she was. "I'm not."

He dropped his head, bringing his lips close to her ear. "Liar."

"Tease."

He chuckled. "I promise, sweetheart. I put out."

She bet he did. And her body was open for whatever service he wanted to provide.

"So, she's only here for Cai?"

Cause she had plans for Cai's daddy, a very big daddy from the hardness of him pressing into her belly.

"Woman," he said dropping a kiss to her lips. "Are you always this jealous?"

She closed her eyes, so afraid of what his touch had unleashed. For years, she'd survived without needing another soul, not Dean, not Trevor, not Johnny, not her father who'd walked out on them, not her mother who almost ceased to exist afterward each man tossed them aside.

"Yes," she whispered, dropping her head.

When Owen cupped her face and lifted, she didn't resist.

"I won't give you a reason, Ivy."

"Promise?" Could she risk putting her trust in another man? She wanted to believe. Wanted to trust Owen, but...

"When the time comes, I'll love you so thoroughly, other women will burn with envy, sweetheart." Her breath stalled. "I promise," he said lowering his mouth to hers.

Ivy arched the slender column of her neck allowing him to deepen the kiss. With gentle coaxing, she opened welcoming his tongue. Sighing with contentment, she wasn't prepared when he thrust deep, angling her head to form a sure seal. This wasn't a kiss, he was branding her, outside and in. As pleasure burst in her mouth, Ivy surrendered. Even as her brain registered a shift between her and Owen, a small voice whispered, *you can't stay*.

CHAPTER SIX

O wen hadn't touched another woman since Caitlyn's death. Now, he couldn't seem to keep his giant paws off of Ivy. He wanted to touch her, erase any trace of Blondie's hands on her skin. Interesting, the boulder that had taken up residence in his chest since the call about Caitlyn's death didn't bear as much weight tonight. Oh, it was still there, but not as crushing. Did Ivy's arrival have something to do with this new sense of relief? He held her hand as they climbed the stairs together. Cai should be asleep, but he knew better. Since Caitlyn's death, Cai needed to see either him or Autumn before he closed his eyes. When they passed the master bedroom, Ivy's steps faltered. He wanted to take her to his bed, but he wanted her to be sure. He never wanted to look at her and see regret in her eyes.

"Owen." Her voice held a hint of question.

Squeezing their intertwined fingers, he tugged her forward.

"Let's check on Cai. He can't sleep until he sees me."

"Oh," she said, a note of sadness infusing the words. No doubt, she was thinking of all he and Cai had lost with his wife's death.

"He's better," Owen reassured her.

"Are you?"

He stopped. Turning, he took both of her hands in his. He told her his deepest hope. "I want to be."

For the first year, Owen hadn't wanted anything to change about his life, even though Caitlyn was gone. Logically he knew she was lost to him, but his heart was lost with her. He'd promised her forever. Forever had been taken away from him after six years of marriage. The only reason he got out of bed that first year was because his little boy needed a father.

"I want that for you, Owen."

He bent to kiss her. Man, she was so giving. He'd never met a woman like her. "You taste so sweet, Ivy Summers," he said raising his head. "Don't change a thing."

"Daddy," Cai's sleepy voice called.

"I'm here, buddy."

"Can Ivy read my bedtime story?"

Owen felt her fingers go stiff. What in the heck?

"What's wrong?" he whispered.

"Nothing," she said too quickly, averting her eyes.

"Daddy, can she?"

Studying Ivy's profile in the soft warmth of the bathroom light, Owen frowned.

"Hold on, Cai." He turned back to her. "Ivy, tell me."

She gave him a shaky smile. "You go, I don't want to intrude."

When she tried to separate their hands, he yanked her into his arms. Was the possibility of a package deal too much for her? This afternoon, when she'd thought of his son, not him, he'd seen something different in her. Other women had expressed their interests in him, but he could tell when they weren't too keen on raising another woman's son.

"He wants to see you."

Her face softened, yet he could tell something was holding her back.

"Ivy," Cai called. "Do you like *The Land of Do As You Please*?"

Ivy looked to Owen for guidance.

"His favorite book."

She bit her lip, and then she succeeded in extricating her hand from his. He wouldn't force her. Any woman that wanted to be in his life had to accept Cai.

Ivy walked, albeit on shaky legs, to Cai's open door. "I...ah, never read that one, baby."

"Oh, wow. Daddy we can teach Ivy. She can't do as she please."

They both laughed. Either Autumn or Cai had pulled the book from the shelf. Cai's room was exactly as Caitlyn had left it. A racer bed, with Ironman drapes and coverlet. Cai wanted the entire room painted red, but Owen had put his foot down at one accent wall. At least, Caitlyn had called it an accent wall when one of the three walls bore a different color.

Cai placed the book in Ivy's hand. She rubbed her hand over the cover as if studying Braille. He watched in confusion when she flipped through each page, lines of concentration marring her pensive features.

"Cai... I might mess up a few of the words, okay," she said shooting a glance in Owen's direction. "I need you to help me."

Realization hit Owen like a frozen slab of beef. She was nervous about reading in front of him.

Cai's eyes lit with delight. One thing about his son, he liked to help.

"Yes," he beamed, clapping his hands.

"Ivy, I could—,"

"I can do it, Owen."

Pride swelled in his chest. She'd shared her vulnerability with him, and he would stand beside her in support.

Moving closer, he placed one hand on her shoulder in encouragement. When she reached up and covered his hand with hers, he felt like he'd won the biggest teddy bear at the Sacramento County Fair.

Ten minutes later the story was done, and Cai was sound asleep. On quiet feet, they exited the room and partially closed the door.

"I'm dyslexic, Owen." She dropped her head in embarrassment. "Was nine-years old before I could read with any fluency."

She seemed to shrink before him. What the heck did she expect him to do, criticize her?

He took her into his arms. "I'm proud of you, sweetheart. It takes courage to confess a difference that others can't see."

Ivy hugged him so tight that his heart broke a little for the challenges she must have faced. Who'd made this wonderful, passionate woman feel less than perfect?

"I like you, Owen Tate."

He chuckled. "Oh yeah?" he teased, raising a brow.

"Yeah," she said, burying her head in his chest. "I do."

"Feeling's mutual," he smiled. "Come on, let me tuck you in."

When she blew out a breath, he knew he'd made the right decision—to go to bed alone. Even now, feeling her willing body curled against his, Owen knew his life would never be the same. Twenty-four hours ago, he never imagined the sense of hope that unfolded on the inside of his heart. Had he found the woman for him and his son?

CHAPTER SEVEN

Ivy wanted to keep Owen with her a while longer. Reading with Cai and admitting her disability to Owen had shaken her. A lot had changed since she tugged on the door to No Limit Bar and Grille. They stood in the entryway to her room. Did he want to stay by her side, too? His fingers tangled in her hair before she felt a gentle tug.

"Penny for your thoughts."

Should she admit that the last thing she wanted was to lay down alone. Ivy had spent most of her life alone. Even growing up in her mother's home, she'd felt so alone after her father left. It was like his absence had created a void in both her and her mother's lives. A void her mother had no idea how to fill.

"I was thinking your hand could use some ice." The lie rolled off her tongue with ease. Would he take the bait?

Relaxed, he slid his big arms around her waist, a peculiar look covering his handsome features.

"Ivy, if you want to stay with me, just say that. No need to create a reason."

She blushed. He must have seen the color change because he chuckled.

"Not used to a man being direct."

She shook her head. "Not with his feelings."

"His feelings? You thinking of a specific man?"

Ivy refused to discuss her past, with anyone. She went still at the low grumble in his chest.

"You can trust me not to judge."

It wasn't his judgment she was concerned with. Ivy had beat herself up enough over the foolish choices in her life. In reality, she didn't want to open Pandora's box, because that heifer talked entirely too much.

"I know." Though she'd known this man for less than seventy-two hours, she inherently knew she could trust him.

"So, you're not ready?"

Her body was ready for everything his touch promised, but her heart needed a little more time.

"I am."

He rubbed a thumb over her lips. Ivy's mouth watered. The feel of his roughened hands against her skin spiked her temperature. What would he do to her with those calloused fingers?

"I want everything, Ivy. More than your body."

She opened her mouth to deny his claim, and he pressed his lips to hers.

"Don't lie." His eyes hardened. "Like I said before, when the time is right, it'll happen between us."

Her mouth, no longer wet with desire, felt dry suddenly. He seemed so sure of her. Ivy gave the saying "by the seat of her pants" a challenge. She couldn't think of a time when she felt absolute in one of her decisions. Flexibility was key to a life on the move.

"Why are you so sure about me?" How could he want so much, when they knew so little about each other?

"You like my hands on you."

Actually, she loved the feel of his hands caressing her skin. Never had a man's touch undone her. His fingers acted like a master control switch. Ivy knew she was powerless to refuse his commands.

"I do," she admitted, not ashamed to share her desire for him.

"You're the first woman, since I lost my wife, who has garnered my attention, Ivy."

Whoa. Had she ever been anyone's first?

Her heart soared at the compliment.

"That's nice," she said, giving him a coy smile.

A guarded expression crossed his face, but then as fast as it had appeared it disappeared. Was he troubled by the revelation?

"Owen, if this is too soon-"

His hands settled at her waist, before he took her mouth again.

"Come downstairs. I need to make sure Autumn closed up the bar."

She hesitated only a moment, before she fell into step beside him.

"Why didn't Autumn come upstairs to put Cai to bed?" Had he said something to the woman? Not that Ivy cared what the babysitter thought of her, but it was never her intent to cause Owen any trouble. After all, Cai would need her once Ivy left. The thought surprised her. But, somehow she knew she would take care of both Owen and his son for as long as she stayed in Endurance.

"I told her we would get Cai off to sleep."

With a squeeze to his hand, Ivy halted their descent.

"Why would you do that?" Owen Tate saw entirely too much when he looked at her with those bottomless blue eyes.

"'Cause, I noticed you watching us."

Her breath hitched. Had her disappointment been that obvious?

"I did no such thing." She so had. He gave her a smirk, and her facade crumbled. "Okay, maybe a little."

"Ivy, I have to consider Cai in everything I do. There can't be any cat and mouse games between us."

That was the thing, though. She felt pursued. His every look, every touch had her acting on instinct, mating instinct.

"Come on. I could use that ice."

The fact that he was hurting jolted her into action. She began to move, with a smooth stride down the steps.

"Does your hand ache?"

"Not my hand, sweetheart," he grimaced.

She frowned. "Then, what is it?"

"My hand is fine, but there's a part of me that's for sure swollen."

She knew it was pure male arrogance that prompted him to divulge his "situation" but joy blossomed inside her. Owen Tate saw her, the flirting, the edge, the flaws, yet he still desired her.

"Yeah," she said meeting his eyes. "I think I could use some ice, too."

Once in the kitchen, Ivy prepped an ice pack while Owen checked the ovens, refrigerator temperatures, tomorrow's menu, and the doors.

With the heating unit dormant for the night, the California chill common to the western desert settled over her skin. Goosebumps rose, and the ice she held didn't help.

Right on cue, Owen entered the room. He studied her and though she felt the cool in the room, her body heated. Taking in the evidence of the chill to her skin, he plucked the bag from her hand, depositing it in the sink at her back.

"Come here, Ivy." His voice struck all the right cords on her sex-meter. God, every cell in her body wanted to be tangled up in this man. Without conscious thought, she walked right into his arms.

"I'll warm you up," he whispered, closing strong arms around her. How had she lived for twenty-two years having never felt the sensations coursing through her body? This man appealed to her in the basest of ways, yet he fed her spirit, her hopes, and dreams.

"Gosh, Owen. What are you doing to me?"

"What does that mean?"

The whole time he kept her close. She couldn't remember her father or her mother cradling her with such tenderness. For the first time in her life, she truly felt cherished and dare she allow herself to think it, loved. Could Owen Tate love a woman like her?

"I can't bear to be away from you," she confessed.

"And that's a problem, why?"

"Owen, be realistic. You'll be judged for cavorting with a woman like me. A nomad with limited education, limited resources, and an unlimited potential for screw-ups." That's when he drew back, leaving her with an empty sensation.

"All I'm hearing is how other people might perceive us. I know you're an amazing woman, Ivy. Is there a reason you can't be with me?"

And there it was. He'd put the decision back in her hands. She could hear the underlying question in his voice. Why don't you want me? Ivy's novelty had wore off quick. The flirting, the sassy comebacks were her weapons. When she was alone, she was just plain old Ivy— a woman with no home, no connections, and no future.

"There are a lot of reasons," she said, not quite sure she could share what happened to her mother at the hands of a lover.

"I want to hear them, Ivy. I'm not walking away from how I feel about you."

Ivy's heart beat a little faster in her chest. Here was this big-hearted guy, well-educated, trusted member of society who'd lost his wife, yet he'd endured that grief in silence and focused on raising his son. Now, by some twist of the universe, he wanted Ivy with all her problems to share in his world. How could she not fall in love with him? He needed to know the truth.

"Owen," she breathed. "My mom and I never had very much. There were times when I was growing up that we had to live in a women's shelter. The Second Chance House in Shell Cove, its home for me," she said not looking at him.

How pathetic she must appear. Who considered a shelter home? Ivy felt the sizzle of his warmth before he touched her.

"You could have a home here, Ivy, in Endurance."

When Ivy looked into his blue eyes she saw compassion rather than condemnation. She wanted what he offered so bad she ached with need.

"My mom had a tough time with men, Owen. A lot of different men," she emphasized without saying more. "As I got older, I began to understood that all the uncles in our life were men she depended on to take care of us. I started looking for opportunities to stay away from wherever we were living at the time."

Owen pulled her into his embrace. "You were a kid, Ivy. You should've been protected from that. It's a good thing you learned to protect yourself."

"I had to look pretty, put on a dress," she hissed. Thinking of how she felt like an object up for auction, Ivy's stomach rebelled.

He stopped her. "You don't have to perform for me, Ivy. I see you and I like what I see," he whispered.

"I know, but-" What if she judged Owen all wrong?

"She met a nice man and I thought she had finally gotten it right. I felt okay about staying away. She was safe," her voice trembled. Ivy had never regretted being wrong more in her life. She suspected she never would.

Owen had picked up on the change of tone in her voice.

"What happened?"

"They got in a fight. He lived to tell his side of the story—my mom didn't."

"Oh, sweetheart," he whispered. "I'm so sorry." He pulled her in close to his chest.

"I wasn't there for her, Owen. I let her down."

"Shh, now." With his big hands, he rubbed her shoulders, and made soothing treks up and down her back. How could he treat her with such kindness? Her mother had been the only person in the world to really love her, and Ivy had failed her.

"You did no such thing."

"I did. She trusted him. I put my trust in a man too-"

"As a parent, I would never want my child in harm's way. She loved you. Trust me when I say your mother was thankful you weren't there that day, Ivy."

Could Owen be right? Could she realize the guilt of having failed the one person who loved her unconditionally? Right now, she could not put the emotional energy into unpacking all the hurt, pain, and loss she felt over the decision to stay away that day.

"Thank you, Owen. I appreciate you sharing your perspective."

Silence stretched between them.

"Not all men take advantage of their women, Ivy." He tugged her hand. "Come. I'll put you to bed."

Guess he'd picked up on her man issues. "Let's not talk about that now."

He pulled back, encircling her upper arms in both hands. Owen looked down, his eyes fixed on hers.

"Then when? I would never hurt you, sweetheart. You know this about me, right?" His eyes lit with determination. She knew the topic would be waiting for her in the morning. "So, what are you searching for, Ivy?"

She'd found it here in Endurance, with a little boy who loved sweet potato muffins and a blue-eyed protector who loved to touch her.

"Nothing you don't already possess."

At her admittance, those determined eyes, softened with satisfaction.

She pleaded with him one last time. "Make the right decision, Owen." She couldn't if he kept touching her. He and Cai had a good life without her. They would be right as rain when she left.

"I did," he said, pressing their bodies together, "now it's on you." Then he covered her mouth with his.

Ivy slipped under his spell wishing she could spend all her nights in his arms.

OWEN could not allow Ivy to push their relationship strictly into the physical realm. He felt her eyes on him, begging him to take her to his bed. Somehow, he knew after everything they'd shared today, making love to her now would relegate him into the same category she used to dump other men. Her body held a definite appeal, the woman was toned and curvy, but he wanted to possess the heart of her. The portion she guarded with bold flirtations and a sharp tongue.

"Get in," he said pulling the cover back.

Wordlessly, she climbed between the sheets. White lacy panties peeked out from under her t-shirt, taunting him.

Next, he pulled the covers over her chest. The rounded globes bounced, and his body tightened at the knowledge that besides the panties, her body was bare beneath the thin shirt. Gritting his teeth, Owen ignored the burgeoning stiffness in his pants.

Small fingers wrapped around his wrist.

"Will you stay with me?"

Just like that, Owen felt his will power slipping away just like those panties she wore would. He could have her bare and beneath him in minutes. It would be so easy, but how long would it take tomorrow to mend what he broke tonight? He wouldn't betray the trust he knew she needed, even if she didn't realize everything she asked of him.

"I'll stay," he offered, but then quickly added, "until you fall asleep."

Even in the shadow of their bodies, he saw her eyes drop to half-mast.

Toeing off his boots, he stripped down to his boxers and shirt and climbed in beside her.

Without asking, he lifted and pulled her lithe form onto his chest. He replayed everything that happened today. Man, Delaney's callout had netted him one of the best days he'd had in years. Ivy had handled the bar and grille with ease, wowed his customers, and put a smile on his son's face. In a word, she was incredible.

"Thank for agreeing to make Cai's birthday cake," he whispered.

When the soft pads of her fingers brushed across his pecs, he placed a palm over her hand, keeping it there. Ivy couldn't know how much that cake meant to him and Cai. Caitlyn's accident had happened the day before Cai's third birthday. She'd promised to bake Cai an Ironman-shaped cake complete with the red outfit. In the aftermath following her death, Owen had been too grief-stricken to deliver on his wife's last promise to her son. They spent Cai's birthday in tears, both of them. Owen lost in his grief, Cai with a broken heart.

"You're welcome," she whispered back, tickling the underside of his hand.

""Go to sleep, sweetheart," he warned, knowing tonight would be all wrong for lovemaking. Seeing Ivy in his kitchen, the sheer delight she exuded at providing a meal for people she liked, told him she was more traditional than she let on. He needed, no...wanted to woo her. Show her and himself he could romance a woman.

"You sure you're not a tease?"

Instead of answering, Owen tilted his hips, pressing his hardness into the fold between her legs.

"Oh," she gasped.

"You still want to play till the sun comes up?" This was a topic that was no laughing matter, and Owen had to address it if he truly wanted a future with Ivy.

"You mentioned leaving in the morning."

"Yeah," her voiced trembled.

"What's so pressing that you have to go?" He took a chance and shared his heart. "Endurance might grow on you if you give her a chance." Now, that he'd put himself out there, he plowed on, hopeful something he said would take root. "There's some good people here. I could help you." *I could love you*, he thought.

She stilled. A moment later her head came to rest on his right pec. "Till morning, huh?" she asked, changing the subject.

"The first time," he challenged. He effectively let her off the hook, because if he took her tonight, he wasn't pulling out until she screamed she belonged to him.

"I'd better rest up."

Squeezing her hip, Owen chuckled. "Good idea, sweetheart. I'll be home later in the morning than usual."

"Why?" she asked, and Owen smiled at her interest in his whereabouts. Ivy Summers was definitely the jealous type.

"I have a meeting scheduled with Abel Burney over on the golf course to firm up the plans for Cai's party on Saturday." The next words he spoke could possibly take her away from him, so he debated whether to mention it at all. "Delaney will be here in the morning."

Owen held his breath unsure if Ivy would take the parachute he'd given her. Again, he had Cai to consider. If Ivy was going to leave, it would be better, he told himself, for her to be gone in the morning.

"Nice, you can introduce me to her and Autumn," she said, sleep heavy in her voice.

A shaky breath escaped him. Owen realized he'd been nervous. The uncertainty of whether she'd choose him and his son or a road to nowhere gave him an edgy churn in his gut.

"Want to come with me tomorrow?"

It only took her a second to respond. "Yeah, I'd like that."

He wondered if it was the fatigue talking but decided to accept the gift of her company for as long as he could. Owen grinned knowing she'd share a ride with him and Cai in the morning.

"After breakfast, we'll drop my little buddy at school, and then our adventure will start."

Ivy yawned, and said, "Stay away from the toaster."

A trace of humor filled her words. As a single parent, he had the sole responsibility of preparing all the meals. He welcomed another set of hands in the kitchen, especially when the food tasted like Ivy's. Her body softened against his and Owen moved to get out of bed. With her hand, she reached out and stroked his cheek.

"Come here," she whispered.

Owen's control wasn't the best on a good day. With her hot little body pressing down on him, his restraint flickered like a candle in the desert wind. "What do you need?"

Voice heavy with sensuality, she said, "Give me a good night kiss."

Owen met and held Ivy's gaze. "If we do this," he said, trailing his callused thumb across her lower lip, "then I'm the knot in your rope. You hold on to me. I won't break, so you don't let go."

Ivy parted her lips, and then stroked the pad of his thumb. Flames ignited in Owen's blood, threatening his self-control.

He threw an arm around her back to pull her up closer, and then he said. "You really are playing with fire."

She grinned up at him. "I'm a Florida girl, remember. I can take a lot of heat."

"In that case, it's whatever the lady wants," he chuckled, covering her pliable lips with his own.

Twenty minutes passed, and her shapely curves went lax in sleep. He heard the slow intake of her breath and knew fatigue had claimed her. Lifting her easily, he placed her beside him and stood to his feet. Owen looked down at the sleeping woman. He knew he needed to get some rest, because Ivy Summers was still prepared to run away with his heart and he'd do everything in his power to keep them both with him.

CHAPTER EIGHT

Open mouthed, Ivy gapped at the expansive Abel Burney Golf Course. Lush greens covered rolling hills with natural bodies of sky blue water dotting the picturesque landscape. In the distance she could see the vast lands of Willis vineyards. Rows of grapes vines planted in precise formation looked back at her, their sugared fragrance more potent in this Mediterranean-like climate. To the east, tall pine trees expanded the verdant canvas as far as the eye could see. The view left Ivy breathless. This small California town, a hidden gem, literally sparkled like a jeweler's display case.

"You look like you appreciate the scenery."

The voice came from behind her. Ivy spun away from the Pro shop's giant window to come face to face with a man.

He smiled, broad and friendly. "I'm Abel Burney," he said, extending his hand in greeting. "I own the place."

"It's the most beautiful place I've ever seen," she said, unable to curtail her enthusiasm.

Abel was tall and lean like a lot of the men she'd seen around Endurance. His skin was the richest tan. With his dark slate eyes and slightly gray temples, he reminded her of a distinguished gentleman. It was easy to see him in a tuxedo or at a fancy gallery or something. Where Owen was rough hued, this man was refined, with a masculine elegance.

"Play a round or two?" He gestured to a golf bag with a few clubs inside. "On me, of course."

When Ivy took a step back, he smiled.

"I couldn't possibly." She'd never touched a golf club. Even now, the only reason she could think to pick the thing up would be to swing it like Tiger Wood's ex-wife.

In two days, she'd met two business owners. She could hardly believe her luck. She liked the town and the people of Endurance. Blinking back what felt like tears, Ivy took in the shop. The space was large, with royal blue carpeted floors, circular clothing racks, ball cap stands, and wood shelves with the latest in Footjoy golfing shoes. Abel Burney had done well for himself. Back in Shell Cove, the men in her eastside neighborhood were grateful to have employment. Owning a business seemed almost foreign to her, yet this man and Owen struck her as born-to-command leaders. And now, in his generosity, he'd offered her a gift. In a short period of time, she noticed generosity applied to several of the Endurance men. Owen had given her a job and a place to stay. Luke and Hank, she knew left tips under their plates that were more than the cost of the meal. Those gestures were a matter of survival. While she appreciated Abel's kindness, she couldn't possibly accept.

"Can't possibly do what?" Owen's timbre came from behind her, filling the room. Ivy jumped, not having heard him enter the golf pro shop.

Apparently, Owen had arranged for lunch in the club restaurant for Cai and his school friends following a morning of miniature golf.

Abel chimed in, "I offered your lady a round of golf on the house."

"Oh, we're not—"

Ready to correct Abel's assumption, Ivy started to tell him that she and Owen were, well...she didn't know what lay between them beyond attraction.

"We'll take it," Owen replied, stepping closer to drape proprietary hands on both her shoulders. She smelled the scent of his minty breath a second before his lips brushed her cheek. "We have four hours before Cai has to be picked up from school. The staff has everything arranged for his birthday party on Saturday" he whispered. "It'll be fun, Ivy."

In a low tone, she warned, 'I've never held a club." She didn't want to be held responsible if she gave him a black eye.

He nestled in even closer. From this position, there was no doubt she and the bar owner were very familiar.

"Let me teach you."

The double meaning in his words triggered a rapid release of raw hunger. Ivy's knees buckled, but Owen was there, holding her, giving her support. Everything about the man made her boneless with need.

Whenever they touched, the connection seemed to transport her to another dimension. One where only she and Owen existed. With a wink from Abel, Owen had her outfitted in a sherbet orange Polo shirt, and a khaki-colored skort. It was the first time a man had purchased her new clothes. Ivy about choked at the eighty-eight-dollar price tag.

"Thank you, Owen, but for that much money, we could've shopped the runway at Goodwill," she responded.

Owen just shook his head, smiling like a teenager who'd bought his girlfriend a promise ring.

The crack of metal hitting plastic resin at high velocity snapped through the air. Someone must be on the course, even though it was barely eight o'clock. Her head sprang up, to find Abel Burney's knowledgeable eyes on them.

As he looked from Owen to her, a slow smile spread across his face. "Well now. Seems we have reason to celebrate."

Oh no, in that moment Ivy wished she'd stayed home. Abel had been so nice to her. When she left, and she would leave, he'd know that she had somehow hurt Owen. Her sexy bar owner wanted more than she was willing to offer. He was the best kind of man; warm, considerate, generous, and protective.

"I think so." Owen's voice dropped low, and she blinked realizing she'd missed some transfer of information between the two men.

Abel offered his hand. "Ivy welcome to Endurance." To Owen he said. "You know where everything is. Enjoy, folks."

Fifteen minutes later Ivy found herself peering down at a hot pink colored golf ball with Owen nestled against her back. Supposedly he was trying to teach her a basic stroke, but her mind wandered to the repeated stroke of his hardness against her back side.

"Concentrate, sweetheart. Stay the course."

Though an innocent request, a spark ignited in Ivy's blood. How was she supposed to focus with him pressed up against her?

"Bite me," she snapped. To her surprise, the feel of his teeth nipping her earlobe sent a bolt of electricity straight to her pleasure center.

Taking a deep breath, Ivy let Owen guide her into drawing back her club face and striking the fluorescent dimpled sphere.

To her delight, the ball took flight. Owen explained the dimpled surface helped with wind resistance.

Three hours later, Ivy's mind reeled at how much fun a stuffy game of golf could be with Owen close by her side.

"Oh my goodness," she laughed. "I'm doing it." Dropping the club, she did an awkward turn and fell into Owen's waiting arms.

He hugged her tight. "Yes, you are, my little amateur."

"Not at everything," she teased.

"Ivy," he growled. Immediately she could feel the air shift to something more carnal between them. "You want to continue last night's game?"

She looked up into his eyes. The predator she'd seen in his eyes before had returned. This time she wouldn't shy away. With both her hands free, she stroked her big cat's back. Before her eyes, those blue eyes darkened, the pupils narrowed to pinpoints, yet she knew she was more in his sight than she'd ever been.

"Walk," he growled low in his throat. The rumble vibrated through the hand she placed on his chest.

"Where?" she asked, glancing around.

Grabbing both her shoulders, he turned her so that her back was to his chest. An outcropping of trees stood about fifty yards off to the left.

"I'll tell you when to stop."

Oh goodness, would he touch her in the light of day? Her heart rate sped up. She struggled to draw in a breath. The thought of being caught excited her. A heavy hand swatted her full backside.

"Ouch," she yelped, rubbing her stinging cheek.

"Stop daydreaming, sweetheart. I'm all about giving you the real thing to hold onto."

And hold on she would. Everything about Owen Tate had been seared into her mind.

They breached the tree line. Ivy expected to find a clearing on the outside. But, it was just the opposite. The trees grew taller and more dense in this area of the course. She should have known. Her protector would keep her safe, even her modesty.

Without preamble, Ivy found herself pressed up against a hard pine, Owen's harder body covering her from breast to hip bone.

"Kiss me," he demanded.

Her lips were on his in a flash. After the morning rush to get Cai off to school, she'd missed her fix of Owen's hands on her.

When he penetrated her mouth, Ivy's body seemed to buzz. A dizzying, its-about-time sensation washed over her. She would never get enough of Owen's taste.

This time when he touched her, Owen's hands found their way over all of her curves. He palmed her breasts, her belly, her derriere. Stopping there, he groaned in her mouth.

"Owen," she whispered.

"I love the way you fill out a pair of jeans. It drives me crazy every time you're within an inch of me. I can't help but want to touch you."

Eyes closed, she tilted her head, allowing him to pepper her neck with kisses.

"You can touch me whenever you want, Owen," she stated, willing to give him anything he asked for in that moment. "I love it when you touch me."

He froze. Desire blazed in his eyes. She held his stare. Her gaze telling him she was his to pleasure. She wanted the same thing he did, to be desired beyond reason.

Lifting a hand, Owen threaded thick fingers into her loose tresses. She didn't flinch when he twisted her locks around his fingers. With a long look and silence, he used his other hand to loosen her buttons on her top. Never had she been more grateful he'd taken her t-shirt away. She moaned when he pulled her swollen mounds, heavy with need, free of her bra.

He looked down at her exposed flesh. As the silence stretched between them, she moved to cover herself.

"Don't," he said, his voice husky. "You're beautiful, Ivy."

There was awe in his voice and appreciation in his gaze. Her breath hitched for the briefest of moments.

Pressing her lips to his, she whispered, "Thank you. You're the best man I've ever known, Owen Tate."

Somehow, Ivy knew sharing herself with Owen would change her life. The look in his eyes, the need, the hunger, the male possession would visit her in her dreams years from now. Sucking in a deep breath, Ivy blinked back the emotion threatening to spill from her eyes. This brooding, demanding, wounded, yet passionate man found her beautiful.

"I'll give you release but, Ivy the first time I make love to you will be in my bed. You deserve that and so much more."

In that moment, she knew the feelings she harbored for Owen were more than lust. It was love. Maybe not the kind in fairytales, but something more flawed and anchored in reality. When he touched her there with his fingers, she communicated with her body all the words she could never say to him.

HIS fantasy of touching Ivy in the most intimate of places paled in comparison to the reality. Unequivocally, she had to be the sweetest woman, the essence of her still flavored his mouth, yet Owen wanted her again. Depressing the gas pedal, the truck rounded Hood Road as they cruised through town. He glanced at his woman lazily relaxed next to him. Her head against the passenger door. He thought her too far away but contented himself with the fact that he'd put that dreamy look in her eyes.

"Feel proud of yourself?" she asked, not looking at him.

Heck, yeah. He'd satisfied her without fully claiming her. Anticipation of the night to come had him adjusting his pants.

"Do I have a right to be?" Not that he required reassurance, but her silence as they left the golf course troubled him. Ivy wanted him, not just for love making, either. But something or someone kept her at arm's distance. He thought back to the trouble that had brought her to Endurance. He'd told her he wouldn't judge. What else could he do to earn her trust?

"Daddy?"

Cai, secured in his safety set, leaned forward, his head appearing larger in the rearview mirror. His son had been bouncing on antsy feet when he spotted Ivy in the car.

"Yeah, buddy."

"Is Ivy sweet?"

From the passenger seat, Owen heard Ivy choke. Reaching across, he patted her back trying to hold his own laughter.

"Yeah," he said, cupping a hand possessively around her neck. "She is."

Every cell in his body told him this woman was his, that with Ivy they would be a family again.

"Is that why you tasted her last night?"

What in the Sam Adams? Owen's foot slipped off the accelerator. The truck speed dropped, and a car horn sounded behind them. He glanced over at Ivy. Wide-eyes stared back at him out of a strawberry-red face.

"Ah, well, you see son. When a man-"

Four-year-olds didn't get lessons in the birds and bees, did they? What the heck did the birds or bees know about craving a woman? What the heck did he know about explaining the kiss Cai must have witnessed in the hallway last night?

Cai sat forward in his booster. "I told Mrs. Petry before nap time that I seen you tasting each other. She said you'd kissed Ivy. Can I kiss her, too?"

Ivy chimed in, trying to change the subject.

"I thought Saratoga Springs would get us home faster?" Ivy asked, a furrow between her brows.

Owen's spine stiffened. He avoided that road. Hadn't lay a tread on the asphalt covering that ground since the day he placed Caitlyn in the ground.

"Should I kiss Ivy too, Daddy?"

Owen could tell by Ivy's pinched expression that she felt uncomfortable with Cai's line of questioning.

"Hey, buddy. How about we discuss this at home."

"But-"

"Just me and you, Cai."

"Okay, but I like Ivy. I should get to taste her, too."

Owen was beginning to feel decidedly uncomfortable on Ivy's behalf. The confusion Cai had to be experiencing wasn't lost on him. How would he explain if Ivy decided to leave? Was he moving too fast? He and Ivy would have to discuss the direction their relationship was heading. As a single father, Owen never planned to parade a string of random women around his son. In his mind he saw Ivy staying with them...forever.

He looked in her direction to find that nervous habit of hers in full affect. Her thumb was firmly pressed into her bottom lip as if she was trying to keep herself from confessing. It reminded him of a child reluctant to tell a parent of wrongdoing. He decided to ignore the comment about Saratoga Springs and reached for her hand instead. They sailed through the intersection of Hood and Saratoga Springs.

"Hey," he said capturing her hand and placing it on his thigh. "You okay?"

Cai piped in from the backseat. "Daddy, you going to taste her again?"

Four-year olds and their fixations. Owen swore the kid just liked saying the word taste. But he pulled on the patience that came with being a parent.

"Cai, no more talk about and tasting Ivy, Mrs. Petry, or kissing."

"Ivy?" Cai called.

"Yes, baby?"

"Can I have some of your unmunchables?"

Ivy's jaw fell slack and Owen choked on his own spit.

"Wh...what?" she stammered.

Owen recalled her very adult joke about her unmentionables with him yesterday morning.

"You told daddy not to put your unmunchables in his pocket." Ivy muttered a few indiscernible words before mouthing the word help. "I asked Ms. Petry if I could have some unmunchables from the snack drawer. She said you two need to start talking in private."

"Cai," Owen warned. "No more questions."

Owen could see a confounded frown on Cai's face from the rear-view mirror, but the inquiries halted.

Turning his attention back to the woman beside him. "Ivy, answer me. Are you okay?"

She pulled her hand away. Had Cai's line of questioning upset her?

Owen encouraged his son to ask questions about the world around him. He never considered curtailing the behavior because it was just the two of them. He wanted the type of relationship with his son where Cai would seek him out for guidance.

"Look, if Cai's questioning upset you-,"

She looked at him. "It's not that."

His first thought was to doubt her statement, but then she smiled, and it reached her eyes. "Ms. Petry's right. We need to be more careful."

Relief washed through him. The way she framed her response meant there would be a next time for them.

"You got it," he said, recapturing her hand and placing it above his knee.

"Daddy?"

Owen gritted his teeth, remembering Cai watched closer than a Catholic school nun. "Yeah, buddy?"

"Since you get to taste, Ivy. Can I at least hold her hand?"

For the first time Ivy turned to face Cai.

"You can hold my hand whenever you want, baby boy."

Cai responded with an enthusiastic string of clapping.

Owen had to ask. "Does this mean you're going to be around for a while?"

She swallowed, and Owen tried not to notice the smooth movement along her slender neck. Tonight he'd use his lips then his tongue to trace her there.

A shadow briefly fell over her eyes. "Owen, it's probably not a good idea, but I'll stay as long as I can."

Owen slid a calloused finger along her jawline, wondering what caused that shroud of sadness to appear behind her normally sparkling eyes.

"Good, because I wouldn't let you leave."

She grinned. "How would you keep me?"

He thought about how she came apart under his touch on the golf course.

"Oh, sweetheart, you forget. I have the stroke to make a hole in one."

She laughed, soft and sweet, and the sound did weird things to his heart. He wanted to hear her laughter in his home, in his life, now and forever.

"Owen Tate, I do believe you're set on playing house with me."

Good gravy, he hoped Cai would think Ivy referred to a game. If he mentioned playing house to Mrs. Petry in the morning, Owen would probably receive a call from that awful school principal before noon.

Now it was his turn to smile. "You can count on it."

Ivy agreed to stay. Now, if he could just get her to tell him why she felt she had to leave them. No one had come looking for her. Tonight, he'd ask about her fears, and pray she trusted him enough to be honest about why she thought to leave Endurance and him behind.

THE NEXT TWO DAYS CAME and went in a dizzying blur of running the bar and prepping for the birthday party. Four days with no sign of Poe didn't make her feel safer. The opposite had taken hold. Why had Ivy promised Owen that she would stay in Endurance? He would expect her to honor her word. Even now, he trusted her to take care of Cai while he got caught up on the books and balancing the bar and grille registers.

Poe said she owed him. The robbery that got Johnny killed had gone sour. And now, Johnny's debt was hers. Poe was smart and vicious. Was he already in Endurance?

Why had she offered Owen a life she had no way of delivering? And more than her problems with Poe, if her relationship with Owen went south, it placed him in a precarious situation with his son.

Owen seemed as uncomfortable as she with Cai's questions. In the past, she had been careful when it came to men. Not that she had any experience with men and their children, but she never wanted to leave Owen alone to explain her disappearance. So, what had she done? Offered a solution that served to complicate matters. Even now, she recalled the hope reflected in Owen's eyes when she'd said that she would stay.

"What are you doing?" a small voice asked.

She turned to find Cai seated in his booster seat at the table. His streaming program must have ended. She found Cai's inquisitive nature refreshing. The fact that he seemed to enjoy having her close by made her yearn for the home life Owen had built in Endurance. The kitchen felt like home to her. Would Autumn bake for Cai once Ivy left?

"Making you something for an after-school snack," she said, placing a lunch plate in front of him. She'd made a small fruit salad with raspberries, strawberries, and a palm sized amount of blueberries leftover from breakfast. Placing a couple of spoonfuls onto Cai's divided plate, she dished the rest into bowls for her and Owen. Cai loved cheese, so she'd taken a slice of sourdough bread made at the Cupcakery and added a thick slice of American cheese. In under an hour three grilled cheese sandwiches and a pitcher of fresh-squeezed lemonade were ready to be served.

"Goody," Cai exclaimed. "What's for lunch?"

She gave his cheeks a light squeeze. A rosy color remained when she released him.

Ivy decided she liked taking care of Cai—and Owen. To wake up every morning and find a loving man and this boy who delighted in her every gesture waiting for her, sent a thrill through her blood. Ivy dared not let herself dream up a reality not meant for her. It was wrong to lead Owen to believe in them being a family. No one counted on a woman like her to stick around, but Owen did. He didn't question, he accepted that she would deliver on her word.

"Ivy," Cai said, half his sandwich hanging out of his mouth.

"Careful, baby. I don't want you to choke. Chew, swallow, and then talk."

When he opened his mouth she presumed to agree, she put a finger to his lips. "Chew."

He nodded. In typical little boy fashion, he opened wide and chomped with gusto rushing to clear his mouth of the offending cuisine. Far be it for food to keep Cai from asking his questions. He was so smart, and she took pride in Owen's child-rearing abilities. To know that he was raising a well-adjusted kid as a single father garnered her respect, and only made her love him more.

An audible gulp came from Cai's recently vacated throat, the sound like a frog's croak. When Cai glanced over as though prepared for a reprimand, a wide smile spread over his cherubic face when he spotted her smile.

"Can I hold your hand now?" he asked.

She took the chair next to his, and extended her hand, palm up, in his direction. When he placed his hand, rounded and small, into hers, she enfolded her fingers.

"How's that?"

Instead of answering, Cai used his opposite hand to tentatively pat her knuckles. The touch left faint circles of melted butter on her skin. Emotion squeezed her heart for all this little boy had lost.

"Did my mommy send you?" he asked, a surreal quality to his voice.

The question so shocked Ivy that she was rendered speechless. Why would he think her arrival had a connection to Caitlyn?

Overwhelmed with compassion, Ivy pushed her chair back from the table and scooped Cai into her lap.

"No, baby. One of my friends, Johnny got hurt really bad. His family wanted me to stay, but I had to leave real fast, so I came here."

Cai rested his head on her chest.

"Did you help him, too?"

On instinct, Ivy dropped her nose to his hair, inhaling the green of grass, the warmth of summer, and the rumbustious nature of a little boy.

"I tried, baby, but it wasn't enough." At first, traveling west with Johnny seemed like the adventure of a lifetime. But, then they'd reached California and moved in with his brother, Poe. It didn't take long for Ivy to discover Poe earned his money through nefarious means.

"I'm no angel, Cai."

"But," he whined, "Daddy said Mommy would send an angel to take care of me."

Unbidden, tears sprang to her eyes. Oh, how he must miss his mother. Though Crystal Summers left much to be desired in the nurturing department, she had been a constant in Ivy's life...until one of the uncles took her away. She and her mother never had a traditional mother-daughter relationship, but Ivy hadn't imagined life without her until she was gone.

"Your dad is right. Mommies have special angels that they share with their little ones."

"I glad you're my angel."

Oh God, how could she tell this precious little boy that she was far from angelic? No one had ever mistaken Ivy's actions for heavenly attributes.

"You're such a sweet boy, Cai Tate. But, I'm just Ivy." She angled her shoulder towards him, leaning down. "See, no wings."

"But if you're not an angel, then that means you might leave."

His voice had risen an octave, and the whites of his eyes began to shine with red vessels.

"Shh, don't cry." She pulled him into an embrace and began to rock from side to side in an attempt to comfort him. "Don't cry. Don't cry."

"Daddy said angels care for us because Mommy sent one just for me."

Ivy heard his sniffles, right before wetness spilled on her blouse, soaking through to her shoulder. "Shh, now. Don't be upset. Maybe, you're right. I'm here."

He lifted his head.

"Really?" he asked, his eyes wide with sincerity.

"Yeah, baby. There has to be a reason I'm here, right?"

Lifting his head from her shoulder, he nodded. Ivy gave him a nervous smile, sure her eyes were as red as his. God, please let her be doing the right thing in reassuring him. What would Owen say once he found out what she'd done?

Cai grabbed her face. "Oh," she stammered.

He kissed her cheek. "You taste sweet to me too, Ivy."

Shocked Ivy looked up to find Owen standing in the archway leading from the small office.

He saw the tears in her eyes, and an indiscernible expression crossed his face. Seconds later he was at her side. He bent and kissed her forehead, and then lifted Cai into his arms.

"You and Ivy, okay?"

Cai looked so much younger in his father's arms. For the first time, Ivy realized she could never willingly walk away from them. Owen must have recognized the change, because he opened his arms and she rose and walked into his waiting embrace.

He pulled her so close, Ivy thought it impossible for anything to come between them.

"We're good," he said to them, but Ivy thought it was for him, too. "Trust me to take care of my family."

And they were a family, each meeting a need in the other.

"Daddy," Cai whispered.

"Yeah?"

Ivy heard the patience and love in Owen's tone. "Now, we can both taste Ivy because mommy sent her."

Ivy felt Owen's hand on her neck, his fingers sliding into her hair. "I know, buddy. Told you Mommy would send an angel to take care of you and me."

Ivy's breath hitched. Did Owen really think her a godsend? She tilted her head to better see his face. When their eyes met, she saw the truth. He believed every word.

OWEN sat on the floor with Cai seated between his folded legs. Autumn would arrive soon, but after the conversation he'd overheard with Ivy, he wanted to hear more of Cai's fears. Since Caitlyn's death, he often asked about Mommy's angel. It never occurred to Owen that Cai would translate Ivy's arrival to being his angel.

"Daddy, Ivy said she's not my angel."

"I heard her, buddy."

"But, she came. And now you and me are happy again."

Gosh, Cai was right. In less than a week his house buzzed with the activity and conversation of a loving home again.

"Yeah, she did that, huh buddy?"

"She has to stay. Make her stay, Daddy."

It was rare Cai allowed him to put him over his shoulder like when he was an infant, but this time he did.

"I'm working on it, Cai," he sighed. "I'm working on it."

Owen had heard Ivy's comment about her friend being hurt, but the chill in her voice said the injury had been serious, maybe fatal. And why did the family want her to stay around if the person connecting them was gone? Was that why she had him pay her in cash? Was she now trying to get back to this family who wanted her to stay. He didn't think so. The woman was definitely running from someone. Whether she knew it or not, now that she'd run to him, Owen swore he'd slay her dragon, and claim his prize. Starting tonight, he'd claim every part of her, including her heart.

"Promise, Daddy?"

"Yeah. And you know your daddy never breaks a promise."

Placing Cai in front of his tablet, Owen pulled up an easy read, and placed the square pad in his hand. "Read. When Autumn arrives tell her all about your story."

"Yes, sir."

Away from hearing distance, Owen dialed up the local sheriff. When Keith Fullerton picked up the line, Owen began as soon as the sheriff rendered a greeting.

"It's Owen Tate. In the past week, have there been any accidents involving a man getting seriously hurt or injured? Maybe between San Diego and Culver City?"

Keith listened as Owen gave him different scenarios. Considering what Ivy had confessed to Cai, she had omitted a lot of detail. Thinking back, he tried to piece together everything he remembered from when Ivy walked into his life. "Guy's name may be John or Johnny."

Keith grunted. "This friendly inquiry got anything to do with the woman living at your place?"

How had the news reached Keith? Owen hadn't seen the guy in a couple weeks. He hated to admit it, but Keith had been the one to inform him of Caitlyn's death. After the way he'd crumbled at the scene, Owen found it hard to face the man. Not that anyone judged him, but he hadn't been available when his wife needed him.

"Didn't realized I'd mentioned that to you, Keith."

"Cut the crap, Owen. Some woman walks into town and you let her shack up at your place. The whole town's abuzz with the news."

Who had spread rumors about Ivy's arrival? Autumn would never betray his trust and Delaney had been MIA.

Owen growled his displeasure. "I don't shack up. Ivy's with me."

"Is she now?"

The skepticism in Keith's voice rubbed him raw. Maybe he needed to make his connection to Ivy crystal clear.

"Yeah, she's mine." Heck, he sounded like a Neanderthal. "If anyone else in town needs to be set straight about Ivy's place in this house, I'll be the one to do it." Anyone who thought to approach Ivy as anything less than what she was, the woman he loved, would answer to him.

"I'll look into this. Expect a visit when I have something."

"A call will do." He didn't want Keith sniffing around Ivy. He had the distinct feeling Ivy would not appreciate a cop paying her a visit.

CHAPTER NINE

Ivy was dead on her feet. It was after one in the morning, when she took to the backstairs, eager to put her head on the pillow. After her conversation with Cai, Owen had disappeared behind closed doors with his son until the evening crowd began to pour in. She had been delivering drinks when he entered the bar. It surprised her that he hadn't sought her out. A sinking feeling settled in her stomach. Had he overhead the discussion she had with Cai? She'd studied his features when he'd taken Cai into his arms. She believed him when he said they were fine. But, maybe she hadn't read him as well as she thought. In reality, he had taken his son and left her alone.

Ivy thought back to this afternoon when she became aware of Owen's presence. He couldn't have been in the room when she told Cai. If he had been within earshot, was it possible for him to piece together the real story from the details she'd shared with the four-year-old?

Hand on the doorknob, she pushed against the wood, putting a little extra power into the move to shoulder the door open. Stepping inside, she froze. Owen sat in the chair by the window. The moonlight bounced off his muscles, making him appear as a male god etched in black onyx. He wore a plain black t-shirt and dark drawstring pants. His feet were bare.

"Been meaning to oil the door hinges. I'll do it in the morning."

Tossing the bar towel from her shoulder to the footboard, she gave Owen a shaky nod. "Okay—thanks."

Owen pointed to the open door at her back. Why was she standing pole still, afraid to move? A quick drop in her stomach signaled the answer. If she went to him tonight, she would be his forever. He'd make sure of it. She lowered her head, closed her eyes, and tried to take in a steadying breath. Her body hummed with energy, every cell on high alert. Owen Tate somehow had become the most important person in her chaotic life. He anchored her, comforted her, and now he would claim her. Would it be too soon if she told him how she felt? Would he want her love along with her body?

"Owen—,"

She heard his exhale. "Close the door, Ivy."

Pivoting, she did as she was told, waiting until the click of the lock carried into the still room, sealing them inside...together.

She swallowed, all of a sudden more nervous than she ever remembered being. "Cai asleep?"

Stupid question. At one o'clock in the morning, the Man in the Moon was nodding off. Of course, the four-year-old deep in dreamland was probably whipping up more questions to unbalance them with tomorrow.

Owen held a relaxed pose in the plush chair. He spread his legs wide and patted his thigh.

"Come here and sit."

Okay, Ivy's belly quivered at the low timbre in his voice. She slid a hand over the smooth skin of her belly to quell the unseen motion. The soft thud of her boots against the wood felt like a slow march into a new life. Owen asked her to trust him? Her history with men and trust lay thinner than an ice glaze under a heat lamp, but Owen had proven to be a man of his word. He wanted her to stay, and she didn't want to go. Where did that leave her? Two words came to mind, with him.

She held up both hands. "Wait," she whispered. "I want to tell you something first." He needed to know about Poe. Why she ran. Why she might have to keep running.

Owen extended his hand, beckoning her forward. "First, you come to me."

She heard the command in his tone, but there was also yearning. It was then she recognized he needed her to choose to spend this night with him. Though he'd entered her room, he wouldn't force her to enter his life.

Seconds later she found herself in his arms, her bottom resting on his muscled thigh. She sighed in contentment. His scent, bold and intrusive, clung to his shirt. Burying her nose in his neck, she inhaled the heady scent, instantly aroused.

He chuckled. "Long day?"

"The longest."

"Sorry, about Cai. I never had a reason to curtail all his questions. Caitlyn, his mom," he paused, and Ivy thought he would stop talking. He rarely mentioned Caitlyn's name. The fact that he had, told her that, though the consummation of their physical relationship was still to come, the depth of emotion they shared was just as intimate, if not more than the act itself. With arms around his neck, she held him tight. Telling him with her body that it was okay. He was safe with her. "Caitlyn used to encourage him to think out loud."

"That's good. I like that he asks questions."

Owen put her slightly away from him. Their eyes met. His rich blue pulling her deeper into his world.

"What?" she questioned after a moment.

"Everything you tell me, no matter what, you can trust me to keep between us."

Ivy didn't like the serious current that edged his words. She stiffened. So, he had overheard the conversation with Cai. "How long?"

She didn't have to say more. He knew what she referred to. How long had he stood back listening to their conversation?

"Long enough. But, I need you to tell me all of it, Ivy."

She dropped her head. Poison Ivy. Everything she touched eventually turned toxic. This situation would be the same.

"Owen, please," she pleaded, not looking at him. Maybe, she should give them this one night without placing an impossible barrier between them? Life could be cruel. Owen was the perfect guy, yet, she was perfectly wrong for him.

She felt the caress to his fingers along her jaw. Gently he raised her chin.

He said two words. "Trust me."

Johnny said the same two words, before he'd walked into that Qwik-Shop and came out on a stretcher.

"Hey," he adjusted her in his lap. "Come back to me, Ivy."

She shook her head ridding her mind of the past. Johnny was gone. She was alone in the world, again. Or, was she? Ivy looked up at Owen. Ivy prided herself on taking life as it was, not how she wished it to be. Realists dealt in reality. But, here with Owen, her sense of equilibrium had turned on its head. He wanted her in Endurance, with him. Why? What could she possibly offer beyond a few good times? Maybe he treated all his lady friends like they had a lifetime of days and nights together. But, she believed him when he said he wanted her to stay.

"I'm here."

"And, I want you to stay...with me and Cai." There was that word again—stay. A permanent home. "Tell me why you're running. And don't insult my intelligence with a lie."

She closed her eyes in surrender. "Five days ago my friend, Johnny was shot and killed during an attempted robbery at a Qwik-Shop outside of Vista."

She waited for Owen to dump her on the floor like a smoking hot turd. Instead, he placed a soft kiss to her lips.

"A boyfriend?"

She nodded, surprised when tears wet her cheeks. Embarrassed, she wiped at the wetness with the back of her hand. "Sorry."

"Me too, sweetheart."

"For what?" she sniffed, rubbing her nose. Gosh, she must look a mess.

"For your loss."

Wow, no one knew that she'd had lost a close friend. When they'd first met, Johnny had been amazing to her, supportive, fun, and non-judgmental. He truly loved her. Maybe, not more than earning his big brother's respect, but she got it. In and out foster homes and juvie, life hadn't been good to Johnny or Poe. While Johnny chose to get help, Poe continued in the cycle of hurting others the way he had been hurt.

"Thanks," she whispered. Appreciative that he sought to comfort her rather than respond with condemnation or jealousy.

"You cared about him."

She nodded, not sure if it was a question or a statement.

"Yes."

"And me? Do you care for me?"

Her breath hitched. There was no way to verbalize everything she felt for Owen. He made her better. Made her want to get her two-year degree in business, maybe a four-year degree like him.

"I do."

He took her mouth. The kiss was deep and demanding. Threading her fingers in his hair, Ivy pushed deeper into his mouth, marking him the way she wanted to be marked. When he nipped her tongue with his teeth, she nearly came undone. This man wrecked her. His touches took her places she'd never been and didn't want to leave. His caring told her he'd always provide a safe haven for her heart. His kisses promised nights of passion and a home filled with little grumps with blue eyes and a sweet tooth.

When Owen broke the kiss, his breathing was as ragged as hers.

"Tell me the rest. Who's after you?" he breathed.

When she thought to keep quiet, he narrowed his eyes. "Either we have trust, or this ends now."

No, she wouldn't let that happen. She wanted everything his kiss promised...tonight.

"Johnny's brother, Poe. He wanted us to rob the store together, but..." Johnny, being the gentler of the siblings, had always wanted to impress his big brother. So, even though Ivy had refused to participate, and begged Johnny to leave with her, he agreed to Poe's plan. "Johnny and Poe went inside. When I heard the first shot, I jumped out of Poe's monster truck and hid. Poe ran out without Johnny and drove away." She swallowed. "I stayed hidden until Johnny's body was taken away."

"Then what happened?"

"Poe circled back after the cops left, but he didn't see me from his vantage point. I hid in a multi-level parking garage that had a view of the store's front entrance. After he disappeared, I walked for a while and then flagged down a trucker and landed here in Endurance."

How long would Owen give her to pack? Would he try to take back the money she'd earned?

"Wrong," Owen said, cupping her face. She frowned. "You landed with me."

"Oh," she whispered.

"I'll keep you safe. You believe me?"

She swallowed. "Yes."

He stood, taking her with him. Owen placed her on her feet, his big hands spanning her waist, steadying her. Once he was certain she had a sure footing, his hands fell away. Turning on the table lamp, he took his seat, leaving her standing alone.

"Undress for me, sweetheart." When she looked at him in confusion. He sat back. "I like to watch."

Oh gosh, he wanted to see her undress. Looking at him, she slowly began to remove her clothes. When she stood before him naked and vulnerable, she wondered would he see beyond the flesh and bone? The flare of heat in his eyes said yes. Owen Tate liked what he saw.

OWEN dug his fingers into the fabric covering the armed chair. He watched as Ivy unbuttoned her jeans with shaky fingers. For her, he would maintain his control. When all he wanted to do was jump to his feet, tear off her clothes with his teeth, and then pour himself into her. She tilted forward, with both thumbs tucked into her waistband. Ivy tugged snug jeans over her full hips, and tiny ivy green panties came into view. Owen grabbed the arms of the chair, willing himself to be patient. They had all night. He should have known Ivy would surprise him.

In no time at all, she had him out of his clothes, his hard body pressing hers into a soft mattress. On the golf course, he'd promised to make love to her in his bed, and he would...later. Then she raised her hips and pulled him into paradise.

Heat and passion, desire and desperation exploded inside, and he lost himself in her. Her screams of pleasure thrilled him beyond measure. Thank goodness, Cai was a hard sleeper. Hearing his woman's satisfaction, feeling her body temperature rise beneath him, and seeing her skin flush in desire drove his passion higher. Owen thought, it would be later, much later that they made it to his bed because there was no way he'd pull away from his slice of heaven before sunrise.

Their bodies moved in perfect rhythm, a sensual dance directed with the drive of Owen's maleness into her writhing feminine softness. The feel of her holding onto him in the most intimate of ways rewrote his imagination. No one would ever measure up to this woman. Intertwining their fingers, Owen wanted her tied to him.

"Let me touch your body, Owen." At the sound of Ivy's whimper Owen hastened his movements. Pushing them both toward that predetermined end. "Owen, I want my hands on you. Please."

Before he completely came undone, Owen released one of her hands. Now free, Ivy dug her nails into his back. Owen growled in encouragement. "More," he hissed, wanting evidence of their lovemaking carved in his flesh.

She obliged him, tightening her muscles, pulling him to new depths just as the bite of pain tingled along his torso.

"Oh, Ivy. If you're an angel, I'm going to hell."

She faltered beneath him. In a tone laden with pleasure she gave a pant. "Why?" she asked, voice hoarse from her screams.

"Because I'm going to do every wicked thing that comes to mind with you."

She grinned. "I hope so."

He freed her other hand. Without his instruction, Ivy locked her arms around his neck. Pulling free of her body, Owen locked eyes with his woman. With his back straight, he gripped her hips and pulled her onto his hardness. She cried out at the abrupt entrance.

"You ready for more of me?"

"Of you? Never. But, I want you none the less," she said, a soft moan trailing behind the words.

That she thought herself ill-prepared floored him. From the moment she strode through his door, Ivy Summers had him wrapped around all ten of her skillful fingers.

"Oh, you're ready," he grunted, stroking their pleasure higher. Owen seized her hips in a punishing grip, using her body. He took what he wanted, giving her the pleasure she begged for with every caress, every nip of his teeth at his neck, every scream echoing around him.

"I'm close," she panted. "I don't want to be alone in this."

She wouldn't. Owen barely maintained his sanity at her wanting him to share in their release.

Leaning, he dropped to his back, pulling her atop of him. Grabbing her hands, he placed them on his chest. "Take me with you."

Moving, Ivy held him captive with her heated chocolate gaze. He looked on, memorizing the mask of pleasure gracing her body, the perspiration between her breasts, his name on her lips. Moments later, her body tensed, stilled, and she screamed out in ecstasy. Owen followed. Taking control, he pushed her into a sensual wave of pleasure, bellowing her name as he drove her to take everything he gave. Ivy Summers was delicious in every way. She was addictive. Even with his body exhausted, he craved another dose of her. Sometime during the night, he acknowledged he'd given her his heart. Now, he prayed she'd keep it safe.

CHAPTER TEN

IVY lazed across Owen's chest, quiet as he twirled a lock of her hair around his fingers.

"Stop playing asleep," he chuckled.

"Who's playing? I had a rough night." She laughed placing a kiss to his bare chest.

He rubbed a hand down her bare waist. "Don't get me started," he crooned, voice steeped with daring.

"I won't. I have to go shopping for some supplies this morning."

"How much did you take from the register, Ivy?"

She propped her bent arm on his chest to support her chin. "Excuse me...what?"

"The books are off by a few hundred dollars. You paid yourself an advance?"

Mouth open, Ivy bolted up. "Owen," she breathed, wounded that he assumed she would take from him. "I don't steal."

Owen pulled her back down to the bed, rolling on top of her.

"Never thought you did. You've been stocking and purchasing supplies. Thought maybe you spent the money on stuff for the kitchen or took your daily pay. I heard you were eyeing the flowery dress in Trina's display window."

This town was full of spies and maybe—a thief. Even though Owen wanted her to stay, he'd held to his word. Every night her online account grew by fifty dollars and he placed a fifty-dollar bill in her hand. The guys had been coming in the bar tipping her on the regular. Ivy knew Owen was curious about the amount of money she collected in tips, but he never asked. She appreciated that he let her do her job and kept his opinions to himself. Instead, he told her how impressed he was with her management and customer service skills.

Ivy had worked a lot of odd jobs. Since joining the team here at No Limit she released she had a knack for hospitality services. An idea came to her. Tonight, she'd use to office computer to check the university course catalog for classes in that field.

"That is something we needed to talk about, too. I don't like the idea of you socking away cash money each day. I want you on the payroll."

"You pay me. I wouldn't take anything you didn't give to me."

He knew that, right? So, where was the money?

"And if I gave you my heart?" he asked.

The very air in the room stilled. Ivy's heart beat wildly in her chest.

Owen hopped out of bed, not meeting her eyes. "Rest. I'll get Cai off to school."

She reached for him, but he backed away. "Owen, it's just...," she trailed off.

"I know. Too soon."

She fell back on the bed. Angry with herself that she'd hurt him. But, how could a relationship like theirs last? A high school graduate with no prospects of a better life and a business owner with an MBA from the University of California. "I'll make breakfast."

When his finger grazed her cheek, she exhaled the breath she didn't realize she had been holding.

She cracked one eye. "Stay away from—,"

Laughing, he barked out, "The toaster. You're in charge of the kitchen from here on out." He chuckled on his way to the door.

Ivy had just closed her eyes, when the door opened again. A smiling Owen crossed the room, threw back the cover, and nipped her ass. "I've been looking forward to leaving my mark there."

She laughed. "You did plenty of marking last night." Her body was deliciously well-used.

The hinges squeaked, and the door flung wide open. "Ivy, Daddy's not in his—,"

Ivy gasped scrambling for the covers. Owen dropped to the bed shielding her body.

"Cai, what did I tell you about knocking?"

Ivy peeked around Owen's back to find a wide-eyed Cai staring from his father to her. She could see all the questions pulling up to the starting line. Poor Mrs. Petry. Owen would have to prepare a written apology after Cai's no-doubt show and tell today.

"Daddy, you had a sleepover with Ivy?"

Ivy held her breath, not sure how Owen would respond this morning to their spending the night together.

"Yes."

Relief swelled that Owen spoke the truth with his son. Certain, that if Owen would have decided to mislead Cai, Ivy would have felt on the outside of their newly formed union.

"So, when can I do a sleepover with Ivy?"

Before he asked, Owen whispered something in her ear that nearly stopped her heart. Could he truly mean it?

Without waiting for her answer, Owen quickly hustled Cai out the door.

"Ivy needs some sleep, so let's discuss the difference between adult sleepovers and kid sleepovers on the ride to school."

After the door closed, she fell back into the pillows, and closed her eyes. Happiness colored her dreams in rainbows. When she next woke up, the door was cracked, but there was no sign Owen had returned. Did she want his heart? Absolutely, because he already held hers, him and a little boy who looked beyond her flaws and saw an angel.

OWEN sat behind his desk reviewing the bar and grille deposits from the previous four days. Autumn stood by the door staring at him. There was more than a couple hundred dollars missing, the final count tallied near six hundred dollars. He'd asked Autumn to come to the office to double check his math but was pretty sure the till fell short. For a second, he considered that Ivy had lied to him about taking the money. After all, desperate people took sometimes desperate, and deceitful actions. Owen quickly dismissed the thought. Everything about

Ivy was genuine and honest. The woman spoke her mind before the possibility of deception ever occurred to her.

"You sure Ivy's not the problem, Owen?" Today Autumn sported a turquoise spandex top, matching tights, and a scowl. "What's that bruise on your neck?"

"Autumn, mind your business."

Though he'd been the one to disclose the discrepancy, he never implied the list of suspects started with Ivy. Ivy and the hickey on his neck were off limits.

"You and Cai are my business," she retorted. "I don't want to see you hurt, Owen. What do you know about this woman? Where did she come from?"

"She's one woman alone in the world. Don't judge her by her circumstances. Trust me, she's a decent and kind person. The hardest working woman I've ever met. Just this morning, she mentioned adding tables and stringing lights on a trellis for an outdoor dining room. Does that sound like a person trying to take from me?"

Autumn frowned. Her expression said he was the biggest sap on the planet.

"She's running, Owen." Obviously, the Endurance grapevine was hard at work. Owen had a new appreciation for the gossip mongering in his town. "A woman like that doesn't choose a town like Endurance. You said it yourself, no one finds Endurance without a few bumps and bruises along the way."

He narrowed his eyes, and then sighed. "I know."

"Maybe, you should let her go."

"To do what?" He pushed away from his desk, standing to his feet. "Cai lights up knowing she'll be here when he gets home."

"And you?" Autumn questioned. "How do you feel when you open the door or enter a room to see her standing there?"

Like a fat guy with a dozen hot Krispy Kreme donuts hiding under the back porch.

"I'm good with it," he said coolly.

"What do know about the trouble she's running from? Not that I like repeating gossip, but...she walked into town," she said arms wide, eyes wider with incredulity.

"I never said she was in trouble," he said, defending Ivy.

"Cai said she only has a backpack with some unmunchables she won't share with him." She shrugged.

Dang it. His four-year-old needed a muzzle.

"I won't hold her past against her."

After deploying to a combat zone, Owen understood the need to put some miles between the past and the here and now.

"Her past could negatively impact your future, Owen. Think about that."

"I have. I am. Shoot, Autumn." He thought of little else. His brain worked overtime trying to figure out how he and Ivy could fit together long-term. For now, they were together, but he and Cai wanted their angel's love forever.

"Don't mind me, just a concerned friend."

She got up to leave. Inwardly, he was delighted to see Autumn and her sound wisdom leaving. But then he stopped her.

"I appreciate your concern, Autumn. It's just I need you to keep your eyes peeled to anything suspicious."

"Besides Ivy Summers slinging her tiny skirt in Rui's face," she hissed and then eyed him like fool don't be stupid.

Rui definitely needed to make a move on Autumn. Anyone with a blind eye could see the professor stopped by No Limit strictly to catch a glimpse of her. Looking at the heat in Autumn's eyes, he now understood the reserved Professor Conner had a good reason to continue his twice weekly visits.

"When I come in Ivy's working the crowd. Have you asked Delaney?"

At the mention of Delaney, he grimaced. "She's been MIA all week. A few of the regulars mentioned seeing her pop in, but I think she's avoiding me."

"So, are you going to fire her?," Autumn said, dusting her palms together. "Good."

"Not exactly." Delaney was a sweet young woman, quiet and impressionable. Autumn and Delaney mixed about as well as oil and water. While Autumn went out of her way to pitch in, Delaney barely pulled her own weight. Maybe, Ivy would forge a friendship. Delaney needed more good influences in her life. Owen noticed she gravitated towards the seedier guys that sometimes visited No Limit.

"Owen," Autumn chastised. "That woman is the worst waitress and an even worse cook."

"I know, but besides her Grammy, she doesn't have anyone."

"That's her fault," Autumn grumbled. "Always taking advantage of peoples' kindness." Owen dismissed that last part. "I'm serious, Owen. At least Ivy earns her keep. She waits tables, cooks, and cares for Cai. But, that Delaney," she huffed, "is a con woman."

Owen cut her off. He had to get to the bottom of the missing money, pick up a few birthday decorations from Trina's, and then get back to Ivy.

"Thanks for stopping by, I'll catch up with you later today," he said absently. There was something he'd left on his to-do list.

He decided against mentioning the missing money to Ivy again. The last thing he needed was to start a fight, when all he wanted to do was pull her close and get lost in her love.

OUT of bed, Ivy showered, dressed, and hurried downstairs. There was a spring in her step, so she took the stairs two at a time.

Seeing Autumn at the table with a steamy cup in front of her, Ivy stopped. Peering over her shoulder at Ivy's halted approach, Autumn turned back to her coffee. So, this was to be their introduction. Fine, Ivy was used to other people, especially women, giving her the cold shoulder.

Lifting the mug to her lips, she said. "I saw the boss's neck."

Ivy kept walking, only briefly acknowledging Autumn's statement. The other woman was behaving particularly cold towards her and she wondered if this was solely about Owen. "Looks like he spent the night nursing a female vampire."

Remembering the red marks she'd left on Owen's skin, Ivy almost smiled.

Ivy shrugged. "Some men are suckers when it comes to women." And, Owen wanted her mouth everywhere on him.

She'd blushed red at his demand that she mark him, but secretly she thrilled when he met her compliance with compliance of his own. He had denied her nothing. Owen Tate was a generous and thorough lover. Seeing the redness left by her teeth and her nails this morning had surprised her. Never had she been so passionate with a man. But, Owen seemed to welcome her uninhibited nature. In fact, the wicked man had encouraged her wantonness twice last night, and once after sunrise. No wonder the hot shower this morning had soothed her achy places. Well, some places couldn't be reached, thank goodness.

With his scent gone from her skin, she wanted something of his to remain with her. A few aches would sustain her...until tonight.

"What about Rui?"

The question snatched Ivy back from her musings. "Who?" she quizzed.

"Professor Rui Conners," Autumn replied, her voice rising.

So, this was the woman the professor was searching for. The professor's need to make haste and Autumn's cold shoulder made sense. Gossip spread faster than soft butter on hot toast in Endurance. Everyone at the university probably knew Ivy had approached him that first morning.

"Oh, yeah," Ivy said, snapping her fingers. "The dark-haired professor who likes to peak over the menu."

Ivy could almost see the woman's hackles rise. She admitted, it sounded a bit weird the way she phrased it.

"I heard you talked with him, and he looked uncomfortable when he left."

Where there was concern when she mentioned Owen's name, that concern had been replaced with heated venom when it pertained to the college man. Ivy could see Autumn poised to strike another blow if she responded incorrectly. She decided to let Autumn in on her secret.

"I'm dyslexic. I talked with the professor about local programs that I might benefit from." The wind instantly left Autumn's sails, and Ivy could see the anger melt away. "That's all we talked about. Adult education."

At that, Autumn raised a brow. Ivy immediately recognized the dual meaning. Looking to Autumn, she wondered what the woman would do next. But then, her shoulders began to shake with laughter.

"And did Rui school you?"

"Not in the least," Ivy reassured. "He dropped in a couple of days ago to grab a cheesy macaroni pizza and give me the website address for the free course offerings. The poor man, according to the town hotline, his sitter is on the verge of resigning due to his daughter's pranks."

"Owen's the only teacher I want. I really like him," she said, trying not to giggle like a crazy woman in love.

"So, you and Owen, huh?"

Ivy steeled her spine, readying herself for an insult. Crossing to the sink, she opened a cabinet, grabbed a cup, and filled it with fresh brew. Turning, she faced Autumn. Sipping on the delicious java, Ivy sighed, and then responded. "Yep. Me and Owen."

"Sounds serious."

"Yeah," she sighed. "Seriously complicated."

"And Cai?"

"I love him." She also loved his father, but that would be too much. "I'm working on something special for his birthday."

"Tomorrow should be a fun day on the course for you guys." Autumn's face remained impassive, like she'd forgotten something sad, but just remembered.

"I should thank you for stepping in," Autumn offered.

Ivy crinkled her nose in confusion. "For what?"

"Normally I'd stop by here after my morning runs."

"Yeah, Owen mentioned that."

Autumn gave a small smile. "He thinks my visits are about the free breakfast, but I pop in before class because I know Delaney needs the help. She's terrible at managing the bar and grille, and her cooking—let's just say that conversation was the best thing on the menu before you arrived."

Ivy laughed at that. "Thanks," she beamed. "I appreciate the compliment. Owen lets me do what I want with the menu."

Autumn nodded as if she agreed.

"Owen is a fair boss, and a great father. He's a good guy who's been through a tough time."

Where was she going with this? Ivy had an idea, but she didn't detect malice from the other woman. Only concern for a man she respected.

"Yep. That's all true," Ivy remarked.

"You though, Ivy Summers," Autumn said, pushing out her chair and standing. "Verdict is still out as to whether you are a good woman."

Not if she was good enough, but a good woman for her friend and boss. Ivy found she liked Autumn Raine. The woman was perceptive, and she took good care of the Tates.

"I don't think I am, but I would sacrifice everything I have before hurting Owen or Cai."

This was the first conversation she and Autumn had shared. She'd spare the woman the details of her past and last night. The true baptism by fire with come soon enough, Owen had asked her to move into his bedroom.

CHAPTER ELEVEN

Owen flung the back door open, not caring when the wood frame slammed against the brick wall. Once in the kitchen he spied Cai running around the table and Ivy standing at the sink, Aria Arie's soulful tune playing in the background. The scene was right, Ivy at home, Cai happy and running around the house, but it felt wrong—especially today.

Autumn peaked her head out of the TV room. "Owen how did everything go at the cem-"

"Not now," he rasped.

"Okay, then." Autumn turned on her heel, disappearing from sight.

Ivy stopped what she was doing to regard him. Initially, she smiled, but then detecting his dark mood, her face fell. He couldn't bring himself to approach her. He could barely stand to look at her. It hurt too much. He hurt too much. How could he have forgotten? This morning while he lay tangled in bed with Ivy, he had an appointment to pick up new flowers for Caitlyn's grave. With Ivy under his roof, under him, he'd lost his focus.

"Daddy, look at the shirt angel mommy made me."

Cai ran to him, oblivious to the strain on Ivy's face.

"Mommy?" Owen snapped at hearing the word. He glared at Ivy. "Did you tell him to call you mommy?"

At his vitriol, Ivy stumbled backwards.

She raised both hands in mock surrender. "Of course not," she said, voice weighted down with concern for him. She could tell by his expression, he didn't want her empathy. Didn't need it.

"Daddy," Cai grabbed his arm.

He stomped toward her. "Let go, Cai," he growled.

"He's not your son, Ivy," he said, raising his voice. "Don't let him call you mommy."

She took a step towards him. "Owen I would never do that. What's—,"

He backed away, as if her nearness burned him. The wounded look in her eyes, nearly felled him. He was hurting her, though she'd done nothing but be here, in his space, in Caitlyn's space.

"Today is the anniversary of Caitlyn's death," he blurted out.

Ivy's face lost its color. She was a smart woman, no doubt she was thinking about everything that happened between them last night. This morning, he'd asked her to move into his bedroom. So afraid of her response, he hadn't stuck around for an answer. And dang it, as bad as his heart hurt for everything he'd lost with Caitlyn's death, he wanted Ivy's answer to be yes. They needed to be alone.

"Owen, I had no idea." She reached for him, but then dropped her hand. "What can I do?"

He cut her a look. "We did plenty last night," he clipped. "Cai, go to your room. Ivy and I need to talk."

None of this was Ivy's fault, yet his soul clamored for him to stop aiming his arrows at her. He could see she felt his pain and that she shared in his anguish. God, he loved her. Even in this selfish moment, he wanted her with him, though the guilt of wanting to reach out and pull her into his arms was tearing him apart.

"But, Daddy. She made a shirt for you, too."

He didn't look down. Instead he added a stern, "Cai, now."

The sob that filled the room, wrenched his heart. He looked down then to see tears began to fill Cai's eyes.

Ivy's soft tone, motherly as it were, intruded on the moment. "Cai baby, go on now. We'll show Daddy later."

Owen heard the growl that escaped his throat. How could she be so compassionate to a child who wasn't hers, when Owen was being a jerk to her? It made him want her all the more...at that realization his self-loathing morphed into anger, at himself for loving Ivy and at her, for being so easy to love.

"Don't direct him. I'm right here. I'm his parent, not you."

Ivy put up her hands. "Look." Her lips trembled in hurt and confusion. "I'm sorry," her voice began to tremble. "I didn't mean to overstep."

"Well, you did." He let his anger hang there between them. Watching as it hit her, knocking the light out in her eyes, and his heart broke right along with hers. Owen crumbled on the inside as tears filled her eyes.

"Daddy, stop," Cai yelled. "You're making Ivy cry."

Ivy stared up at him, pain unlike any he'd ever witnessed filled her eyes. But, he couldn't give in to her right now. He hated himself too much.

"I'm going to go for a walk to get some fresh—,"

He cut her off. "You're right. I can't talk about us. I need to work some things out in my head. Just go," he heard himself say.

In his mind, an emotional flood of epic portions roared for him to not let her go, but he couldn't work through his grief for Caitlyn with Ivy within arms reach. He'd used her to soothe his pain, and he'd promised he would never take advantage of her love for him.

"No," Cai wailed. "Don't leave, Ivy. Daddy," he cried.

Owen scooped his son up in his arms. Everything that happened today fell squarely on his shoulders. He was the one that had veered off course. It was his fault his son ran around the house excited about wearing the tie-dye shirt Ivy had created special for his birthday. Owen thought about Caitlyn and what she would've done if she were in his shoes.

"Okay, then," Ivy said, turning to let the water out of the sink. Owen was mad at himself, mad with Ivy. Most women would have run from the room in hysterical sobs. Not his Ivy. She would never break, not like he had. She was so strong. Stronger than him at this moment, because every nerve in his body signaled him to go to her, tell her how bad he was hurting, but he was too weak. Too afraid he'd break down like he had the night he'd gotten the call that Caitlyn had been struck by a car.

These last few days, he'd been living his life...and somehow he'd forgotten everything he planned in honor of Caitlyn's legacy. One thing was for sure; Caitlyn never would have made the people she loved cry their eyes out. How could he forgive himself—he'd disappointed the two most important women in his life.

OWEN placed Cai's limp body on his Ironman pillow. For the first time in months, his son had cried himself to sleep, but not because he missed his mother. No, he cried because Owen had told Ivy to leave them alone. Today was the two-year anniversary of Caitlyn's death and Owen had forgotten. Last night, he'd lost himself in another woman. This morning he'd woke feeling like he'd won a hidden treasure, because of Ivy.

The call from All In Gifts & Flowers, reminding him to pick up the fresh bouquets he'd ordered for Caitlyn's headstone, had spilled a vat of acid in his gut. What kind of husband forgot the day he lost his wife? The kind who had fallen in love with another woman. He'd resented Ivy in that moment. Resented himself for loving her. After visiting the gravesite, he'd returned home to find his son, the only child he and Caitlyn would ever share, calling Ivy mommy. Shame and guilt had slammed into him. He'd failed Caitlyn in life. And now, he'd betrayed her in death. He'd unleashed his pain on Ivy.

Why did he have to care so much for her?

He shouldn't have these feelings for a woman he'd just met. But, he did.

Even now, he wanted to go downstairs, find her, and apologize.

All of sudden, a whimper sounded from the bed.

"Mommy," Cai sobbed, "send my angel back."

Though his eyes remained closed, tears ran down Cai's pale cheeks.

Owen's heart crumbled. Ivy loved Cai and he loved her. What a jackwagon Owen had been. Now, his son was heartbroken, and Ivy was probably downstairs pissed at him.

Dropping low, he placed a kiss to his son's temple.

"I'll get your angel back," he whispered. "I promise."

In a flash he was closing the door behind him to descend the stairs. He'd just entered their small kitchen, when Autumn called out from the television room.

"You should have told her about the anniversary."

Owen gritted his teeth. He liked Autumn, appreciated everything she did to help out with the bar and Cai, but he didn't need a lecture. He needed to find Ivy and beg her forgiveness.

"I will," he pushed out.

"I think I would have grown to like Ivy Summers."

Owen ran a frustrated hand through his blond mane, and then he froze. Autumn said she would've liked Ivy.

Dread, thick and tarry, dropped in his gut. He turned to look at Autumn. Sadness, fresh and vivid filled her eyes.

"Where is she?" he said walking towards her.

Autumn shook her head. "I don't know."

"What do you mean you don't know?" he barked. "What did she say?" he ground out. In the background, an actor on the television cried over some African prince who'd been thrown over a waterfall by his enemy, Killmonger. Owen was experiencing a similar drop. His stomach felt as if it were being trampled beneath a farm tractor.

"You went upstairs. A minute later, she grabbed her backpack from the corner and walked out. She didn't say anything."

Pain, unlike anything he'd experienced since learning of Caitlyn's death cut through his chest. Oh God. He covered his mouth with his hand, afraid his roar would topple the house.

Think, Owen. Where would she go?

Would she walk out of Endurance? Yes, she would. He and Cai were her only reasons to stay, and he'd practically shoved her out the door.

"Thanks," he said, not feeling the least bit grateful for having heard the news that Ivy may have left him.

Owen pulled his keys from his pocket. She couldn't have gotten far. It was getting dark. A ball of unease coiled in his gut. Walking in the dark wasn't safe. Caitlyn had been doing the same thing when she was struck by a hit and run driver.

Just then, the bar door scraped open into the kitchen signaling someone had entered to the private quarters.

"Ivy," he called, feet already moving in that direction.

"Nope."

It was Hank's voice.

Owen's face fell. "Can't talk. Need to find Ivy."

"She's the reason I came looking for you. A fella came in earlier this morning asking about a Poison Ivy. He described our Ivy to a tee. Delaney heard him, too. Surprised she didn't mention it."

Owen frowned. When had Delaney been in the bar? She hadn't been to work in days.

"Did he give a name?"

Hank scratched his chin. "Can't say that he did."

Owen turned to head out the back door.

"But," Hank added as a side note. "His truck made one heck of a racket when he tore off down the road."

Blood roared between his ears, and his brain numbed. Poe. Ivy said he'd come for her. And, Owen had left her unprotected.

He ran. "Call the sheriff. Tell him a man named Poe is after Ivy."

Fury and every protective instinct he possessed roared to life. "I'm going to find her."

He didn't stop when Autumn called his name. He'd find Ivy. He had to.

THE moment Ivy heard Poe's truck rumble down the street, she stripped off the apron she'd taken to wearing, grabbed her backpack, and exited the back door. She ignored Autumn reclining on the couch in the television room.

If she opened her mouth, emotion would overwhelm her, so she said nothing. She took to the woods behind the bar, careful to stay out of sight. She wanted to tell Owen, but there was no time. Would he think she'd cut out on him?

For the first time, Ivy understood that loving someone meant staying the course, even through the tough times. She'd seen the calendar on the refrigerator, next to Owen's cell number that first day in the office. She hadn't realized the significance of the red circle around today's date. Too late, she'd deduced it was the anniversary of Caitlyn's death. Owen had to be hurting something fierce. After she got some place safe, away from Owen and Cai, she'd call him, maybe. Owen had thoroughly refused her offer of comfort. Had he changed his mind about them being together? She sniffed, yet another man with his smooth talk and broken promises. For all her running, she'd been recast in her mother's role over and over again.

When she arrived on the Abel Burney golf course forty minutes later, the front nine holes were clear. She slowed her pace from the jog she'd used to get on the other side of the woods to a steady trot. Hopefully, she could reach the clubhouse before being spotted.

Hiding at the course had been a burst of genius. Laying low at any of the shops in town would've had Poe in her face within minutes. She swore the town had a Harry Potter toilet bowl highway. No way, would an idiot like Poe think to look in the tranquil setting of a gentleman's sport. Seeing that the service entrance was empty, Ivy hoisted her pack higher on her back and sprinted toward the dark corridor.

"Owen's worried about you."

At the sound of Abel's voice, she froze. His voice echoed from somewhere above her head. She looked up to find him standing on the balcony overlooking the woods separating his property from the town of Endurance.

"Is he here?" Please, no. Blood rushed through her veins. Would she have to make a break for it? Owen would probably try to stop her. A part of her wanted him to beg her to stay, but Owen had his own demons to contend with. No need for Ivy to add her ingredients to his pot. Since her mom's death, no one had cared about her welfare. Her survival depended on her alone.

"Nope," Abel said truthfully.

She released a sigh of relief, ignoring the pang of disappointment swirling in her chest. She couldn't have it both ways.

Five days and their time together was over. Even if she could stay, Poe would keep coming for her.

"But, he'll circle back here before long."

Eyes narrowed in suspicion, Ivy took cautious steps, back-tracking her trek through the forest. "Why? Why would he come back?" She knew. Knew that Abel, seeing her stumbling through the woods at sunset, would alert Owen.

"Come inside, Ivy." He descended the stone staircase from the second floor and came to stand before her on the patio. "Don't run from your family."

Her temper, fueled by the pain of Owen's rejection flared. "He's not my family. I'm sure the news will reach you soon enough, but Owen made it very clear what my role was in his life. He doesn't want me, Abel." Ivy swallowed the ball of despair that swelled in the back of her throat, threatening to cut off her airway. She would always consider Cai, with all his questions family...Owen, too. But, Ivy had what she came to Endurance for, enough money to get home, her real home. "Besides, I have friends who'll help me start over back home in Shell Cove." At least she hoped that to be true. No one knew she planned to return.

Tears gathered in her eyes. She wanted to be his, damn it. Wanted to wake up to his kisses and Cai's questions.

"He would disagree with you, as would I. You have friends here, too."

Abel settled a hand on her shoulder. "Let's get those scratches cleaned up," he said pulling her forward.

The man missed nothing. Forgotten was the spill she'd taken trying to climb over a downed tree. The root system had been massive and the limbs still wide and spindly. Since he wanted to help, Ivy walked in front of him, lengthening her stride, like this whole encounter was her idea.

"I'm hungry, too."

Abel chuckled. "Owen mentioned I needed to feed you if you showed up."

Her stomach knotted. Even though he'd told her to go, Owen still thought to take care of her.

Once inside, Abel settled her at one of the tables with a view of the golf course.

"Sit tight." He gave a comforting smile. "I'll whip us up a couple of sandwiches."

The moment he was behind the swinging doors, Ivy ran for the front of the building. If she kept up this pace, she could make it to the highway just after nightfall. She'd hitch a ride in the first big rig heading in either direction.

"I'm so sorry," she whispered after him. Abel would be hurt when he returned to find her gone, but this was the only way. She loved Owen, Cai, and this little town called Endurance. Owen wanted to protect her, but she wanted to protect him, too. Her mother's words came to her. Ivy could take care of herself. Poe would bring trouble to No Limit, to Endurance, and to her new family. She couldn't let that happen.

CHAPTER TWELVE

Once again Ivy found herself on Saratoga Springs Road. The street was fairly well-lit, but she stayed in the shadows. Less than a mile into her journey, it would be a while before she could flag down a trucker headed out of Endurance.

Lights hit her back, but it was too dark now for even her shadow to make an appearance. That's when she heard it, the rumble of the big engine. Her heart leaped in her throat.

She took off at a dead run. Careful to keep to the shoulder, her foot slipped but she didn't go down. No scared girl, trip and fall stupidity allowed. She had to get away from Poe.

The truck slowed. "Poison Ivy," he called, menacing laughter in his tone. "I saw you, darling. Come on out."

He was trying to trick her into revealing her location. Ivy kept moving.

"You know that bar and grille got robbed tonight." Her steps faltered. Oh no, had anyone gotten hurt? "Not enough to cover what you owe me."

Tempted to yell she didn't owe him anything, she sank her teeth into her bottom lip. Keep quiet, Ivy. Car exhaust floated to her on the wind, polluting the air with a smoke-like stench.

"Thing is, an eyewitness saw you take the money. Probably got the sheriff looking for you right now, Poison Ivy."

An eyewitness? Who would help Poe frame her for a crime she didn't commit? The name came in an instant, the disappearing Delaney. Several of the customers had mentioned her stopping by the bar.

Ivy's ankle rolled at an odd angle and twisted. She yelped in pain, too late, she slapped a palm over her mouth. A bright handheld like swung her way.

"Got ya."

Ivy saw Poe's silhouette illuminated by the small light of the truck cab. Quick, she righted herself. Ankle be damned, she took off at a dead run. Her chest heaved as sweat streamed down her back. She prayed the glued heel stayed in place.

"Stay away from me, you wacko nut tart."

The truck engine stopped. "You know I love your pillow talk."

At the mention of the word pillow, Ivy wiggled out of her backpack and sprinted down the highway screaming.

"Fire, help. Somebody, please."

The sound of boots pounding against the asphalt spurred her to push all her energy into moving her legs faster. She pumped her arms and breathed in through her nose just the way her track coach had taught her. It seemed as if sound came from every direction, but she was too scared to look behind her.

Caught off guard, strong arms tackled her, yanking her off her feet.

"Got you," said a man's voice.

Not yet Ivy thought. Allowing her body to go limp. She might only get one chance to free herself. Centering her courage, Ivy bent her knee and waited.

OWEN was just about to release Ivy when he felt her body go limp. He'd pulled his truck onto Saratoga Springs Road and cut the engine. Caitlyn had been killed on this road, and he wouldn't allow the same fate to befall Ivy. If Ivy were on her way out of Endurance he could intercept her, and that's when he'd heard the roar of a heavy-duty truck engine, spotted the flashlight, and knew Ivy was in trouble.

Owen started running. He tore down the grassy shoulder like his life depended on it. Ivy brought renewed life to his everything. He wouldn't lose her and never would she be taken from him. She was running so fast she didn't see him. When the beam passed the area she had been, Owen wrapped her in a bear hug and pulled them into the tree cover.

His breath, fast and deep, sawed through the cool air. He felt the cold wetness clinging to Ivy's skin.

She'd fainted before he could catch a breath. He was just getting ready to lay her down when like mallet, she swung her leg backward, aiming for his knee. The little hellion had been playing possum.

At the last second, he angled his leg. The crumpling blow catching his thigh. "Dag nab it, Ivy."

She tensed. "Owen?"

"Yes," he hissed through the pain clouding his brain.

The flashlight beam pointed at them. Owen pushed Ivy behind him and dropped into a defensive stance.

Poe stood about five feet away. The guy looked like a military tank with a face. His baldhead loomed huge in the dark night, like a planet rotating on a too small axis. In that moment, he had to acknowledge Ivy's bravery in defying this man. Poe made Blondie from the bar look like Steve Rogers before the Captain America makeover.

"Country boys got to learn not to bring fists to a knife fight."

Owen heard the click of a blade, and then a wicked long silver vampire-slayer stake appeared in Poe's right hand.

Real slow, Owen reached into his waistband and withdrew his gun, aiming it at Poe. "I didn't."

Poe lowered the knife. His eyes held a pretentious smirk.

"The woman behind your back is a thief. Robbed your bar."

Ivy stiffened at his back.

"Don't think so, Poe."

"Oh yeah, so she told you about me. Then you know she ran off and left my brother. Before you go risking your life over an illiterate street walker the likes of Ivy Summers, there's even an eyewitness to the robbery."

"Owen," Ivy whispered. "I didn't—."

"Quiet, I got this," Owen said, keeping his eyes on the threat.

"That's right, Poison Ivy. You're on your way to jail. That's where women like you belong."

Before he could stop her, Ivy was from behind his back. "Oh yeah," she taunted. "You belong bent over a bar of soap."

Funny. His woman didn't back down from a fight and he never wanted to change her, but he could handle this. Out of the corner of his eye, he saw the metal glint of a gun barrel reflect in the moonlight. Lightning fast, Owen grabbed Ivy, covering her with his body.

"Hey," Ivy screeched.

"Drop your weapon."

Owen lifted his head to find Sheriff Fullerton and one deputy, both with their guns trained on Poe. The sheriff came to stand in front of him, facing off with Poe.

"I'll pump your good-for-nothing carcass full of hot metal, scumbag. Now, drop...the...knife."

The sheriff enunciated each word.

"She's not worth the trouble," Poe growled, spitting at their feet.

"Says the man who came looking for her," Owen smirked. "Get him out of here, sheriff."

"Will do," Keith said giving them both the once over. "You got, Ivy?" the sheriff asked tipping his hat, in Ivy's direction.

Keith kicked the knife away, while the deputy had Poe raise his hands above his head, nice and slow.

Owen looked down at Ivy. Brown eyes wide with relief, fear, and love. "Do I have you?"

"Answer your own question, Owen. You told me to go."

Right.

"I'm sorry," he whispered.

"You should be," she responded.

He pulled her into his arms. When she didn't immediately react to his touch, Owen placed a kiss to the top of her head.

"Forgive me, sweetheart...please," he breathed.

He pressed Ivy into his body, sharing his heat, his heart. In that moment, Owen realized that he would always love Caitlyn, be grateful for the life they'd created in his son, but he was truly lost in love for the woman in his arms.

"I can't ask you to take me on, Owen. You have Cai to think about."

"I love you, Ivy Summers," he said cupping her face, "I'll give anything you ask except your freedom." Bending, he took her mouth in a bruising kiss. When she didn't immediately respond, he threaded his fingers into her thick tresses. "Kiss me back, sweetheart. Let me taste you."

"Owen," she whispered, a note of anguish in her voice.

The uncertainty crushed his heart.

"I lost Caitlyn on this very road to a hit and run driver," he stated.

"Oh, Owen-"

He held up a hand. "Let me finish." Gathering his courage, he pressed on. "I didn't have any say in how I lost her, but...with you, Ivy Summers, I do. I can't let you go, sweetheart."

Her eyes widened and even in the dim light of the moon Owen saw the doubt in their depths.

"Maybe one day our timing will be better, but until-"

Owen thought their timing perfect. She'd walked into his life when his only reason for taking another breath loved Ironman pajamas and bar-b-q breakfast toast, extra crispy. With Ivy by his side, Owen wanted to live again. He saw her round with their child, him teaching his sons and daughters to play golf, and Ivy teaching them how to love and laugh. They'd add the patio dining behind No Limit at the mouth of the forest. If she agreed to stay, he'd build her a house with a kitchen big enough to bake a thousand sweet potato muffins.

"Do you love me, Ivy? Enough for a lifetime together, a few brothers and sisters for Cai to bombard with questions?" His actions had opened the door for doubt to creep in. If it took his lifetime, he'd make it up to her.

"Now and forever," she said, arms sliding around his waist.

"Good, then you'll have no problem moving back in with me tonight and being my wife."

"Yes," she grinned. "That sounds doable."

"He chuckled. "Not doable, sweetheart. Done."

She nodded in agreement. Owen's pulse leaped in his veins at the knowledge that Ivy would be forever his.

"I love you, Owen Tate. With all my heart."

"I promise, Ivy. I won't hurt you again." Owen had never spoken truer words.

EPILOGUE

Upon Ivy's return to No Limit last night, Cai had refused to sleep in his bed. Though Owen had promised to love her all night long, he settled for holding her as Cai snuggled against her chest, thumb in his mouth, fast asleep. She had to admit the reality of having a family of her own was heady. So, this was what happiness felt like.

Saturday started with more activity than usual. Endurance buzzed with the news of Delaney being in cahoots with Poe. Ivy chose to focus on her family and their day on Abel's course. Balloons hung from the clubhouse balcony. The staff had strung the banner she made with the words, Happy Birthday Cai, spelled out in tie-dye. Her sweet baby boy had jumped about three feet off the ground because the colors matched his and Owen's t-shirts.

"You're incredible," Owen had whispered in her ear.

Ivy purchased that floral print dress from Trina's especially for Cai's birthday party. She wanted to look pretty for her two men. The Sierra Nevada mountains looked majestic in the background, the warm summer air held the faint scent of ripening vineyards, and the man she loved felt solid around her.

Owen cuddled her backside, his head resting on her shoulder. "What do you think about us getting married?"

She smiled, delighting in the flutter of her heart.

"I think I need a real proposal. You on one knee and a ring."

"That's right, Ivy. Make him do it right," Hank said from one of the picnic tables Abel had added outside the pro shop. The whole town had turned out for the party. She guessed Owen knew the party would be huge. There was no guest list; this was Endurance after all. Luke and his daughter Shiloh were competing in a sack race against Hank's boy, Elliott and Jose's eight-year-old, Lupita. Amelie and Cherron arrived together, with Doctor Chadwick Winters, the town's pediatrician and single dad to a two-year-old named James. Rui Conners had shown up late with Simone. Oddly enough, Autumn was nowhere to be found.

Owen groaned. "I swear, he has a bionic ear and maybe one eye."

Ivy chuckled. "What's your answer, Owen Tate?" She turned and embraced him. "You going to do it right?"

"I thought I was," he said, with a wink.

She blushed at the hidden innuendo. "I'll tell you my answer later," she said, kissing his lips.

"I want an answer now," he said, frowning.

Before she could respond, Cai came running up.

"Did I miss it, Daddy?" Owen pulled Ivy to one of the benches under a giant oak. "No, buddy. I buttered her up for you."

Ivy looked between the two of them, not sure what was going on.

Owen dropped to one knee at her feet, and then Cai joined him.

Tears swelled in her eyes.

"Daddy, she's crying already. Did we do it wrong?"

"No," Owen whispered, never taking his eyes off her. "We're doing it just right, son. Go ahead."

Cai pulled a small round sphere, like the kind you see in gumball machines, from his pocket.

He thrust it at Ivy. "Open it," he insisted. "It cost Daddy a lot of money. He said I better not lose it or—,"

Owen clamped a hand over his mouth. "Remember, that's man talk, buddy."

Cai nodded, and Owen uncovered his lips. Cai smiled up at her. "Sorry, I can't tell you what men folk say while Daddy's around," he chirped.

"Of course, baby," Ivy reassured

She couldn't take her eyes off the one-carat princess-cut diamond ring staring back at her.

"Ivy?" Owen whispered. "Sweetheart."

She knew he wanted an answer, but she had a hard time believing he loved her enough to offer forever. Ivy Summers, the little girl who lost everything, the woman who had nothing, was now on the cusp of having it all.

"Ivy, are you going to marry us?" Cai whispered.

The trembling started with her lips. Covering her mouth to hold back the sob threatening to ruin the party, she nodded. Secure that she could give father and son the answer they wanted, she smiled, broad and wide.

"Yes."

Owen jumped to his feet, sweeping her up in a bear hug. "Yes," he repeated. "You said yes."

"I did," she choked out. Looking up into Owen's blue eyes Ivy knew she'd taken her mother's life and her love for granted. This time Ivy would hang up her walking boots. She'd appreciate this chance to give love and be loved. She'd stay the course to enduring love. "You make me so happy, Owen Tate, she breathed, hugging his close.

Cai yelled and started jumping up and down. "Everybody," he screamed. "I got an angel mommy for my birthday."

Ivy's mom had been right, there was a time to endure, a time to stand, a time to strike out on your own, a time to change directions, and a time to stay the course.

The END

Thank you for reading STAYING THE COURSE. So if you enjoyed Owen and Ivy's story, please do me a solid by leaving a review for Staying The Course. https://amzn.to/2Hy02LR

Just in case you're wondering, there are 4 books in this series. Next up is GOING THE DISTANCE. https://amzn.to/2P7cIgJ

GOING THE DISTANCE

Want more Men of Endurance? Here's an excerpt from The Men of Endurance series, GOING THE DISTANCE.

The "risk it all" student. The "play it safe" professor. An improbable pair, but there's no textbook for love.

Music major Autumn Raine is used to taking care of herself. So, when an eight year-old's prank brings her face-to-face with her secret crush, she's grateful for the rescue. But, this close encounter has Autumn wishing for private lessons.

After a failed marriage, single father and college professor, Rui Conners was committed to raising his daughter alone, but Autumn is bandaging his wounded heart one smile at a time. What's the problem? She has no idea he's interested and Rui's relationship with his ex-wife is far from ancient history. How will these two people used to flying solo, find the perfect note to make their duet go the distance?

Chapter One

E arly morning in Endurance was the perfect time to put some extra miles on the pavement. With sweat dripping down her face, Autumn Raine turned onto University Boulevard, giving her muscles free rein. Breathing in, she pulled the cool mountain air deep in her lungs, using the adrenaline high to pump her arms and legs harder. Eight months ago, she'd relocated to this northern California town in the foothills of the Sierra Nevada mountains from San Diego. Though not as verdant as the east coast of the United States, the rugged peaks, majestic grape vineyards, and four-seasons Mediterranean climate held a certain magic for Autumn. Life here in Endurance, where city hall held the town's only post office and the public library shared the same space as the art museum, was beautifully simple.

For the past six months, she started her days with ten training miles. Known for its spawning hills and mountain trials, tourist flocked to Endurance every year for extreme sports. In three weeks she'd face the ultimate challenge, a one-hundred-mile race through the California hill country. In reality, she faced two difficult races, the second a lot more daunting, earning the twelve thousand dollars to cover her tuition costs. In some ways, Autumn was in the race of her life. She had a future to secure.

Ignoring the burn, which she referred to as energy, Autumn tuned into the music flowing through her earbuds. Music had always relaxed, so she let the soulful voice of Aria Arie loosen her muscles, fill her thoughts, and fuel her body to move. In her mind she saw her stride lengthening and the cells firing in every part of her body. Power hummed through her body, she was in her zone.

As she approached town, people started to appear on the street. Julie, the Sport Complicate reporter, was attempting to pedal her bike up the hill on Dodger Lane. Probably on her morning coffee jaunt. With her sunny smile and inquisitive eyes, the full-figured beauty had made progress in her physical fitness. Autumn scanned the area for Abel Burney. Abel owned the golf course here in Endurance and she suspected Julie owned his heart.

The second she rounded the corner on Hood Lane, Autumn stumbled to a halt. She tried to process the scene unfolding before her. A girl, somewhere between eight or ten, sat behind the wheel of a little blue sedan. Autumn's little blue sedan. As a child, Autumn loved to pretend. Pretend she was a singer, pretend she stood on a stage in front of her audience, pretend she drove a fancy car with a loud engine. Well, this little cutie, with twin braids hanging down her back and brown eyes narrowed in concentration, was turning the key. The grind of the ignition, a stark contrast to the quiet of morning. The potential deadly consequence of the moment instantly sent her into action. The engine caught, the soft hum of the motor, spurred her to action. Autumn shot forward, quickly yanking the door open. The would-be car jacker startled.

"Hey," she yelled cringing away from Autumn. "What are you doing?"

The nerve of this kid. She slid her hand over the steering wheel, turned the key, and disengaged the ignition. The small engine dropped back into slumber. Where were this girl's parents? Dressed in a red and blue striped shirt, blue jeans, and sneakers, she looked like a girl scout.

"Where's your mom?"

"In Europe?" she said snatching her arm away. "Where's yours?"

Autumn's entire body reacted, this little girl needed some serious supervision and a whooping.

Using as stern a voice she could muster, Autumn said, "Get out of the car, now."

The little hellion shifted, then stilled.

Hitting Autumn with a narrow-eyed gaze, she asked, "Are you even an adult?"

Mouth open, Autumn couldn't believe the audacity of this kid. "Of course, I'm an adult."

"You look kind of little to me." The kid gave a smirk.

At five foot two, Autumn accepted her petite frame may appear juvenile, but her curves did not. Sputtering, Autumn felt inclined to defend herself. "Well, I'm not."

Not the best come back, but she wasn't used to verbal sparring with a pre-pubescent child.

"How do I know you're not trying to take the car for yourself?" she charged.

What the sugar plum fairy? Autumn was about to lose her religion. Considering the closest church congregation gathered in Pine Valley, twenty-five miles north of Endurance, it might take her a year or two to find it again. For the most part, the people of Endurance kept their own counsel. The practice suited Autumn just fine. She and God had an understanding. He stayed out of her way, and she returned the favor in kind.

"Who are your parents, young lady?" Autumn insisted, adding a touch more authority to her voice, in hopes that the child would come clean. Not that she would call the cops, but still the girl needed a stern talking to.

"Noneya?"

Autumn couldn't recall an Endurance resident named Noneya. She was good with faces, not so much with names.

"Noneya who? What's your last name?"

"Business," she supplied, brown eyes sparking with defiance.

Autumn lifted her hand, finger leveled at the school-aged comedian. The sheer fact that she was an adult should have motivated the child to cower. Autumn leveled a cautionary gaze on the kid.

"Maybe a visit to the sheriff will locate Mrs. Noneya Business."

Long dark brown lashes dripped low, before a furrow formed between her brows. Good, time to end this charade. Autumn needed to drive back to her one room studio apartment, get cleaned up, and then turn around at get back to the university before her first music history class.

"Wait. My dad is inside. He asked me to warm up the engine." She paused a beat before adding, "Yeah, that's it."

Autumn could tell the girl was warming to the lie. "He's teaching me to drive because he's in a wheelchair. He lost his leg when a coyote attacked him on a camping trip."

"You're too young to drive." With a roll of her eyes, the kid dismissed Autumn's comment like she had time and wisdom on her side.

"I'm eight," she said, her tone communicating her disappointment that Autumn failed to recognize maturity when it graced her presence. "And, my father needs help," she sniffled.

For a second, Autumn wondered if there was any truth to this story. Quickly, she glanced over her shoulder. Peering through the large window into High Altitudes Coffee House she spotted Cherron, the local baker and talking with Ivy Summers, Owen's Tate's fiancée. Not wanting to entertain the tale any longer, Autumn replied, "Sounds terrible and painful."

The miscreant had the audacity to bat her lashes in hopes of drawing sympathy. "Yeah, it's been hard on me."

"When did it happen?"

The double blink came in sets of three. Autumn had to give the kid her props. She was creative. How long would it take the little thespian to spin another tale? "When?" she croaked.

Ignoring the guilt that swamped her at egging the child on, Autumn fought to keep a smile from gracing her face.

"Yes. I mean an injury like that takes a long time to heal."

"Huh...yeah. He's been home all week."

Not bad for an eight-year-old's imagination.

Autumn gestured for the kid to get out of the car.

"Come on."

There was no movement from the vehicle. Man, this kid was ballsy. When she was this age, she jumped if she thought her parents wanted her to do something.

"My mom and dad said to be afraid of strangers."

Autumn's patience wore thin with each passing moment.

"Get out from behind the wheel of that car, right now young lady."

Enough already. This kid needed a disciplined, but gentle hand, maybe.

All of a sudden, a scream rent the air.

"Stranger danger, stranger danger."

Autumn spun around looking behind her to assess the threat. People were staring at her and the horror movie scream queen in the car. "No, I don't want to go with you. Please, lady. Leave me alone."

What in the sugar plum fairy?

"Hey," someone called from behind Autumn. Between the raised voices and pounding footsteps, she was more than aware of their growing audience. "Get away from that kid."

Autumn heard someone say they were calling the cops. Oh my goodness, she should have kept running. The kid starred in her own off-Broadway drama and Autumn was the villain.

Autumn threw up her hands. People walking on both sides of the street stopped to watch the unfolding drama.

Sure enough, the door to the sheriff's office opened.

Giving a glance at the kid, her eyes stretch wide when the sheriff slid a hand over his weapon.

Autumn on the other hand wanted an authority figure to get to the bottom of this kid being unsupervised. Whoever the parents were, they needed to be put under the jail. This kid should be in school. The town sheriff was a regular at the local bar, No Limit Bar and Grille where Autumn babysat the owner's son, Cai Tate. Owen was a single dad who used her services on a regular basis.

"Hi, Autumn." The sheriff's light brown eyes crinkled at the corners when he looked past her and spied the would-be car thief behind the wheel. He grimaced.

"Simone, shouldn't you be in school?" asked Keith Fullerton.

"Sheriff Fullerton," Autumn said bewildered. "You know her?"

The sheriff released a long-suffering sigh. "Yep. Afraid so," he said, tilting his tan cowboy hat with a leather braid back on his head. "I have a long history with Simone and her antics."

The squeak of the door closing drew Autumn's attention. Simone, that's what the sheriff had called her, stood in front of the closed door. The kid offered the sheriff a sappy-sweet smile.

"Ah, sheriff. I was just heading off to school now."

Autumn watched to see if the sheriff would let her off the hook. His face looked down right pained. What was going on between these two?

"I told you if I caught you again, I would call your father."

Simone's eyes widened, a panicked emotion covered her face.

"No, don't call him."

The sheriff extended a hand. "To the station with you. Your father can pick you up."

Chin lifted, Simone folded her arms over her small chest.

"Suit yourself," the sheriff said, dropping his hand. "Autumn, follow me down to the station."

"What? Why?" Autumn rebelled, diplomacy out the window. She supported the democratic process, let every voice be heard, but not if it took another second out of her day. Her landlord had given her until this morning to catch up her late payment. This little rebel was the least of her worries. Autumn had rent to pay.

The sheriff looked at her. "A dozen people heard her screaming you tried to take her."

"It's my car," Autumn exclaimed, not believing the entire situation. "I have class in like...twenty minutes."

Without a word, the law enforcement officer pushed past her, picked Simone up off her feet, not stopping when she squealed.

"My daddy, he doesn't care. Don't call him."

For the first time since this very bizarre exchange, Simone's expression was that of a sad little girl. Just like that, Autumn knew she was staying to see who this kid's father was. He was getting a big piece of her mind.

Keeping reading GOING THE DISTANCE: https://amzn.to/2P7cIgJ

Also by Siera London

The Bachelors of Shell Cove Series

- Chasing Ava
- Convincing Lina
- Catching Rebecca
- Claiming Janna
- Second Chance Christmas
- Blindsided: A Lady Guardians Crossover Novella

The Forbidden Series

- Forbidden Distraction
- Forbidden Attraction
- Forbidden Vow

The Lunchtime Chronicles Series

- Whipped
- Thick Cut
- Prime Ripped

The Fiery Fairy Tales Series

- Chasing Flames
- Concealing Fire

- Commanding Heat

The Men of Endurance Series

- Staying The Course
- Going The Distance
- All Out of Love
- Enduring Christmas

The Kelvinian Warrior Series

- Cindra: A Paranormal Cinderella Tale

Detective MaKenzie Young Series

- The Last File

CONNECTING WITH SIERA

Siera London is the USA Today Bestselling & Award-winning author of contemporary and paranormal romance, romantic suspense, and crime fiction. She crafts stories of diverse characters navigating the challenges and triumphs to find lasting love. Intelligence, wit, emotion, drama, and romance are between the covers of every Siera London novel. Siera lives in Virginia with her husband, and a color patch tabby named Frie.

If you like communicating via text message, Text EZSIERA to 474747.

If you want to see my travels, and my grandbabies, as well as my book updates, sign up for my newsletter: https://landing.mailerlite.com/webforms/landing/i2s4f9

And, I'm on social media, too.

Facebook Author Page: https://www.facebook.com/authorsieralondon

Amazon Author page: http://amzn.to/1Oce1Ht

Goodreads: https://www.goodreads.com/siera_london

Bookbub: https://www.bookbub.com/authors/siera-london

Twitter: https://www.twitter.com/siera_london

Instagram: https://www.instagram.com/sieralondon

Pinterest: https://www.pinterest.com/sieralondon

Website: https://www.sieralondonauthor.com

www.ingramcontent.com/pod-product-compliance
Lightning Source LLC
Chambersburg PA
CBHW050748250626
47155CB00005B/1976